HOW TO SURVIVE YOUR MAGICAL FAMILY

CLARE RHODEN

ODYSSEY
BOOKS

Published by Odyssey Books in 2022

www.odysseybooks.com.au

A Cataloguing-in-Publication entry is available from the National Library of Australia

ISBN: 978-1922311436 (paperback)

ISBN: 978-1922311443 (ebook)

Cover design by Elijah Toten

ALSO BY CLARE RHODEN

The Chronicles of The Pale Trilogy

The Pale

Broad Plain Darkening

The Ruined Land

The Stars in the Night

PART ONE
TOBY

CHAPTER 1

THE STREET CAT INCIDENT

WEDNESDAY

A particular way with cats was the only magic I got from my father. I was mostly a dog person, so cat magic wasn't all that much use to me. My sister Helen scored a whole heap of practical skills. Making traffic lights change green, checking how much food was in the fridge, imagining a parking spot into existence, or turning off the iron after she'd left home, that sort of thing. But I was stuck with this really boring, but completely reliable, skill. I could charm any cat to come to me.

Any cat.

Bashed-up old street-wise tom cats, pretty little Persian kittens, world-weary ginger dams, mad-skittish Ragdolls, and fat, haughty Scottish folds, you name it. Yes, big cats too. I didn't even have to sweet-talk them; I just showed up at the zoo or the range. Lions and leopards, cheetahs and jaguars, panthers and tigers. From inside their perfectly created so-called natural enclosures, they came as close as they could get to me and rubbed their foreheads against the nearest wall. If the wall hadn't existed, they'd have pushed their heavy skulls against me, begging me to pat them.

As I said, not a very useful piece of magic. I tended to avoid cats in general and zoos especially. Cats just reminded me that my father handed down only the shabbiest, least profitable iota of magic that any wizardling could want.

Sadly, the feeling was not mutual. Cats kept coming to me.

So, the night we were driving home through the rain, and my sister braked hard to avoid the collision in front of us, it was no surprise that the first thing I saw was a tossing bundle of feline fur. The car that hit the cat stopped for a few seconds. I could almost hear the driver sighing with relief: Phew, only a street cat—that's what she was thinking. She felt just bad enough, or was maybe just squeamish enough, to steer around the raggedy mound of road victim before she sped off.

My sister Helen yelled obscenities at the other driver. She was so good at swearing that you could be forgiven for thinking it was a magical skill, too. Then she flicked on her hazards and blinked a couple of times, in that focused kind of way, into her rear-vision mirror. I looked out of the back window. Sure enough, the flashing blue light of a police vehicle was pulling up behind us. With our safety from other drivers secured, we both stepped out onto the wet road. At least the rain had eased a bit.

Helen went directly to the mangled cat, which was mewling like every banshee of Ireland in an eerie-noise-making contest. As I feared, it was a new young mother, stupidly trying to take her kittens one by one across the four-lane highway. A back-up chorus of kittens was wailing from the verge. By the time I looked down, three pathetic scruffs of wet fur were grabbing at my ankles.

'See to them, would you, Toby?'

Sometimes I resented the way Helen took charge. Usually I was just grateful to her. This time, it was a bit annoying because that was exactly what I was about to do. I didn't always need to be told, but it wasn't worth arguing about.

I bent down to gather the shivering kittens. They were so small that they fitted into one of my hands. I bundled them inside my t-shirt, tucking it securely into the waistband of my jeans, where they huddled in a ball of wet fur that soaked through the material in no time. I knew that looked ridiculous, but at least they were safe.

Their frantic mother was another story. I squatted down beside Helen, who was trying to contain the stricken animal. The skinny black cat batted at her, claws drawn. The fourth kitten was still in her mouth, crying pitifully.

'What do you think?' I didn't like the look of her lying there in such a strange, twisted position.

Helen shook her head. 'Poor love, her back leg's broken. She's in such a lot of pain. I can't do anything until she lets me touch her. Toby, speak to her.'

I looked over my shoulder at the police constable, who'd come to see how we were getting on while his colleague directed other drivers around us. In general, it wasn't a good idea to talk to cats when someone outside the family was listening. Helen, who pretty much always knew what I was thinking, stood up with a smile at the policeman and took him a half-step away. I went down onto one knee, bending low until I made eye contact with the cat.

'Tenner,' I whispered to her, 'your kittens are all safe. Let me have Littlest, let him join his littermates. I've got them all here, tucked in my pouch. Pink and Footsie and Wart, they're all safe with me.'

Okay, so I could read cats' names too. I blamed my dad. His middle name was Felix, which was the only other inheritance I got.

And by the way, no cat ever called itself Felix.

Tenner stopped in mid-screech. She stared at me hard and then blinked. I saw the fear in her eyes fade, and with a sigh she released her ferocious grip on Littlest. I scooped him into my shirt too, where he clutched his siblings energetically, making a good few claw marks on my belly as he did.

I whispered to Tenner. 'Your leg's broken, little mother. My sister can heal it and stop the pain, but you have to let her touch you. Think you can do that?'

Tenner was panting. *You too*, she sent to me, twitching her nose.

'Okay.' I laid two fingers gently on her side. 'Helen, can you help me lift this cat?'

'Sure.' Touching the policeman confidingly on his shoulder, Helen explained that we would take the cats to the nearest veterinary practice. Then she came back to us. Crouching beside Tenner, she placed her palm on the cat's side and gave a strident whisper: 'Ready! Set! Gone!'

Tenner started, her skin rippling up and down the length of her, before she leaped to her feet. All four of them, sound as could be. I grinned, standing in time to take Tenner's bound into my arms. I could sense the relief and the joyous communion as mother cat and kittens fumbled to smell each other through my shirt. We headed back to Helen's car, where I set the little family into the footwell of the passenger seat, resting on the old crocheted blanket from the back. I was carefully placing one foot on either side of them when Tenner looked at me, her eyes glinting green and hard.

One more.

'One more? Tenner, you only have four kittens.'

Catlike, she just stared at me. 'Helen, wait a moment,' I said, backing out of the car. 'I just need to have a look around.'

My sister, bless her, was never uncooperative just for the fun of it. 'Sure, Tobes. I'll just move the car off the road. Then I can wave goodbye to that cute police guy.'

While she drew the sedan over to the side of the carriage-way, I walked slowly along the wet verge, scanning the asphalt where Tenner was struck, listening for any mewing. There was no sound other than the slick swishing of tyres on the rainy road as the traffic sorted itself back into its usual pattern. There wasn't even any blood. In the gutter, though, was a silver bracelet.

The bracelet was pretty battered and bent, but it looked like solid silver. I considered picking it up. It had a charm clipped on it, in a kind of round shape. But I was searching for something alive, so I walked right on, scanning the verge. Nothing. I turned back toward the car.

Passing that shining bit of silver again, I could see that the round charm was actually in the form of a cat, and the bracelet was more of a bangle and not so battered as I first thought. When I turned to look at it a third time, the round cat charm was seated upright on top of the bangle, looking directly at me.

I gave in. I'm not my father's son for nothing. Okay, cat plus charm plus silver equals magic. Though why Tenner thought this was a kitten ...

I picked up the bangle.

Oh. It wasn't a bangle at all. As I reached toward the silver, a shining pulse ran through it and I suddenly had my arms full of tabby cat.

The bangle wasn't just a bangle. It seemed that Katkin (her full name is Katerina, but she likes the short form) had been looking for me for quite a while, magicked inside the bracelet. Tobias Felix was the person she'd been looking for, and as soon as she rippled back into cat form, her voice started in my head.

Tobias Felix, do you know how lucky you are? Tobias Felix, do you know how magical you are?

Well, maybe now I did.

CHAPTER 2
A DOG PERSON

I've always said that I was really a dog person, but our family never had a dog. There were never any dogs in my life, really. But I liked them because I never needed to avoid dogs the way I tried to keep away from cats and zoos. Dogs never embarrassed me by bouncing up to me or barking at me or following me. Not like any nearby cats, which rushed over to me, meowed loudly to get my attention, and did that trippy-flippy, self-satisfied feline trot as they came after me whenever I tried walking away. Then, likely as not, they'd stretch out a paw and hook their claws into my jeans, or even my ankle.

Cats could be demanding. Even before I walked back to Helen's car, Katkin was taking charge.

We should sit in the back. Tenner needs room for her kits.

I saw no reason to disagree with this. Maybe living with Helen made me amenable to following orders, or maybe I immediately recognised Katkin's superior sense of what the stressed road victim needed. In any case, with Katkin perched half-way up my shoulder, I opened the back door.

'What's up?'

'Another cat. Tenner told me,' I said.

She gave a huffing noise and crunched through the sedan's gears more quickly than they appreciated, diving into a small space in the oncoming traffic. As usual, there were no complaints from the other drivers. Helen and my father often told me that everyday magic—the useful sort, that is—was just a matter of good timing and paying attention to signs and signals that other folk ignore or don't notice. Helen had this down to fine art and drove around town and bush, freeway, and avenue with what looked like the utmost unconcern. She was good at holding complex conversations as she motored along, and this time was no exception. Once she was settled, she fixed my eyes in her rear-view mirror.

'Another cat? Tenner?'

Katkin batted her head repeatedly against my chin, purring loudly. *Hello hello hello,* she chanted. *Hello, Tobias Felix! Hello!*

'Tenner is the little mother cat. This one is, um ...'

'What, Tobes? Another kitten? The father?'

Katkin turned and stared at the back of Helen's head, motionless for a few seconds, before she returned to rasping her head against my chin. *Father!* she said good-naturedly. *Wait till we get home. I'm too beautiful to be anyone's father.*

'Are you? I haven't even seen you yet.'

Katkin nestled into the crook of my neck. *So happy!* she said, and promptly went to sleep.

'Tobes?'

It was difficult to bring my mind back to my sister's questions. 'Sorry, Katkin was talking to me. This cat, I mean, the extra one. Katkin. Tenner's kittens are Wart, Pink, Footsie, and Littlest. Littlest is the biggest one, the one she was carrying.'

'Cat names make no sense.'

'They do to cats.'

'Huh.'

We drove for a while in companionable silence, the windscreen wipers making the only noise. Katkin slept on, every now and then flexing her claws into my t-shirt. In the fitful light of the street lamps we passed, I saw that she was a silvery-grey tabby, quite small for a fully grown cat, and that she had at least one white paw. It was hard to tell, but I couldn't see that she was in any way remarkable. Katkin looked like an ordinary, common-or-garden domestic short hair. I couldn't see her face, because that was tucked under my chin, but I imagined huge lambent eyes, delicate whiskers, neatly defined black stripes, and a sweet pink nose. I later found all this to be true, except that Katkin's nose was black.

Helen sighed. 'So, stop smiling at that cat and tell me more.'

I grinned at her in the mirror. 'I will, but I want to talk to Dad first.'

'Oho!' Helen said in her best wizardly voice. 'Do I detect the fragrance of *magic* in the air?'

'Later, sis, okay? Now, what are we going to do with Tenner and family? You told that cute police guy we'd take her to the vet.'

'Yeah, he was cute, eh?' Helen changed lanes, heading for the southbound exit. 'I think home first. It might be that Tenner has her own plans. Another matter we'd better consult Dad about. And Flax, I guess.'

'Yep. For sure.'

Flax is my father's cat, a huge Maine Coon, and the only cat in the world not very interested in me. But then, if you had my father's complete affection, you wouldn't be on the lookout for other sources, either. My dad's whole love was everything any creature, animal or human or spirit, could wish for.

As we turned into the long driveway that led to our house, I wondered what my father would say about our decision to bring home five stray street cats, let alone one magic bangle cat. Then Dad's thoughts about Tenner and the kittens receded from my mind. I started to wonder what Flax would say about Katkin.

CHAPTER 3
CAT NAMES

Helen never understood cat names. She regularly rolled her eyes when I spoke about the neighbour's cats as 'Wit' or 'Fall'—she always called them what their people have named them: Loki and Ewok.

I kept telling her that cat names had meanings, quite important ones, even though I'd never totally worked out the logic they use. There was one type of name that Miss Tan, my English teacher, would say is irony: Tenner's largest kitten being called 'Littlest', for instance.

There was also a literal side that sometimes felt really heavy-handed, and that Miss Tan would definitely have circled in red if I put it in an essay. I would have bet, for example, that Tenner was either the tenth kitten of one litter, or the only kitten of her mother's tenth litter. Our neighbour Mr Miller's cat Wit (Loki) was white (a literal name), but I'd never understood the cat logic behind the name of his other cat Fall (Ewok). It was something to do with honey, Fall said, but it still didn't make much sense to my un-catlike thinking. At least I knew the right name to call him.

Helen, who was very like our mother in many ways, had

only the smallest affinity for cats, and my father sometimes teased her about that. However, she had such a breadth of practical magics that the teasing didn't amount to much.

Dad never teased me. There was nothing to joke about in a wizardling with no wizardry. He was much more likely to look at me with resigned acceptance and a minimum of interest, unless he was giving me one of his 'just pay attention, magic is not that hard' lectures. At those times, he sometimes spoke with animation and enthusiasm. But Dad had pretty much given up trying to develop my imperceptible-if-not-completely-absent latent powers. I was pretty much shut out of their magic conversations, sitting around like a film extra with no lines to speak.

A slightly bored look was the most congenial of the responses I ever had from my dad's cat Flax. Most days, Flax walked past me as if I didn't exist. Mind you, he didn't care much for my sister Helen either. He just treated us both as if we were part of the house fixtures and fittings, not worth a second look. Any ordinary bird alighting in the garden was of much more interest to him, and that would just get a passing glance. The only thing Flax cared about was my dad.

But all of that changed when I pushed open the front door with my shoulder, cradling Katkin under my chin. An enormous, champagne-coloured ball of fluff hurtled madly into the hallway. Flax.

He came to a halt, his claws ripping across the floorboards, right at my feet. For the first time I could remember, he looked me straight in the eyes, his own wide yellow orbs sparkling with excitement. Then he spoke, his deep voice resounding in my head, the first time I'd ever heard it. It wasn't quite a shout, but every syllable pounded out its own exclamation mark.

WELL! DONE! YOUNG! STER!

I was so stunned that I almost dropped Katkin. At the

internal boom of Flax's voice, she pulled her head out from under my chin and made that unmistakable squirm cats do when they want to be put down. Yes, the quite painful one that involves launching themselves away by claw power. She landed neatly beside Flax and they touched noses. *Flax!* I heard, and *Katerina!*

They pressed their foreheads together, and though I could sense there were words passing between them, I was shut out of the discussion. Then Flax peered around my legs and lifted his nose in a dismissive gesture. I understood immediately that I had to go back to the car and help Helen with the street cat family.

Helen was bending over the passenger footwell, speaking gently to Tenner, but the little mother cat was having none of it, her mouth opened in a snarl, her skin-and-bone body tensed to attack. Helen looked up with relief.

'Oh, there you are! She won't let me near.'

'It's okay, I'll get them.'

Tenner subsided at the sound of my voice, but I could tell she was pretty stressed out. It was always best to take things slowly when you had a distraught cat in your vicinity. If you valued your eyes and your skin, that was. I squatted beside Helen but made sure my weight was leaning back, away from the furry family.

I spoke calmly. 'Now then, Tenner, we'd like to take you inside our house. We can get you dry and warm and fed, and then you can feed the kits.'

Not going inside.

'Nobody will hurt you.'

Not inside. Danger.

'Not here, I promise.'

'What is going on?' Helen asked, a little impatiently. She

was, after all, standing huddled in the rain. 'Can you manage? Should I get Dad?'

'If you want to,' I answered, smothering a surge of resentment that Helen thought I couldn't handle one small, needy cat. I stamped down on my annoyance because it was important to stay calm in the face of Tenner's fear. I kept my voice low. 'I think I can convince her.' Even though I hadn't been very convincing so far. 'She's scared, you see. Maybe she's had a bad time inside a house.'

'I'll get Dad.' Helen shrugged her parka hood higher and hurried toward the open front door.

I sighed. 'Tenner, I want to help you. Your kits are cold and hungry. Let me help.'

Stay here. A small pause, and then she said in an even smaller voice: *Scared.*

'I promise you'll be safe. Nobody will harm you.'

Tenner hunched her shoulder, turning her face away. I saw her shiver, a convulsion of cold and fear. My heart clenched, pity and anger roiling under my surface calm. Someone had hurt this little cat, badly. I resisted the temptation to put my hand out to her and instead let out a soft, easy breath. A little triangle face pushed out from under Tenner—Littlest, the big and hungry kitten, wanted *warm* and he wanted *eat*. Tenner pointed her little black nose at me.

Frightened. Hungry.

'I'll look after you, I promise. Nobody will harm you. You're safe with us.'

Trap.

'No, no trap. You can leave anytime you like. There's a cat door, I'll show you. Just let me lift you—you don't need to move. I'm going to pick up this blanket with you on top. With everyone on top. There!'

Cradling my unwieldy armful, careful not to tip the kittens

off their perch, I got slowly to my feet, trying to keep a perfect balance. Suddenly, my father's hand was on my back, steadying me.

'Good work, Toby,' he said. 'Bring her inside. That's one brave little cat you have there.'

Tenner twisted her head to look at him over my shoulder as we walked slowly into the house. I could sense the anxious tension in her body, and she shuddered uncontrollably as we passed through the doorway. My father seemed to understand her fears—of course he did—and he left the door standing wide open. There was no sign of Flax or Katkin. Instead, a cosy cat basket was set against one wall, with bowls of water and shredded chicken meat nearby. Though I wasn't expecting such a welcome for my street cat family, it didn't totally surprise me. My sister Helen, and my father. Always with the right thing at the right time. They were an awesome duo.

I made no comment, but lowered myself to my knees so I could place the fur-full blanket into the basket. As I moved away from her, Tenner's eyes went wide and her limbs stiff, and for an instant I thought she was going to bolt for the door. Cautiously, my father dropped to one knee, a few feet from her, and made a hushing sound.

'Rest easy, little mother. You're safe here. We'll let you alone awhile. Eat, drink, look after those kits of yours. They're beauties. Call Toby if you want us. You are welcome to come and go as you please.'

Tenner blinked, testing the comfort of the cat-bed, then looked out the open door. The kittens began fussing, and with a little shiver, she turned her attention to them.

My father stood, unhurriedly, and pulled at my elbow. 'Toby,' he said, 'we need to talk.'

CHAPTER 4
MY DAD FELIX

Redmond Felix Dartin, my father, said 'we need to talk' whenever he had something horrible to tell me or to ask me.

As far as I was concerned, 'we need to talk' equalled 'you're not going to like what I have to say'.

I followed him into the kitchen with a sinking heart. Part of me wanted to stay in the draughty hallway with the street cats, but I went without a word. I was preparing myself in case he planned to deliver any bad news about those same cats. If he intended to shepherd them back onto the street once they were warmed and fed, then I had a good mind to go with them. Well, as long as Katkin would come with me.

Then I started to worry about where Katkin had got to, but as we pushed through to the toasty warmth of the kitchen, I could see her curled in front of the Aga, right near Helen's feet. Flax was sprawled on the easy chair in the corner, contentedly washing his immaculate self, one shapely hind leg pointing skyward. Neither of them took any notice of us as we came in. I slid into a chair behind the table, and my father went over to the bench where Helen was preparing some food for dinner.

'Sandwiches?' he asked, disapproving surprise in his voice. 'I thought you were going to buy us something special on the way home.'

'We never got to the shops,' said Helen. 'The car in front of us had an accident, in case you hadn't noticed.' She pointed her buttery knife over her shoulder in the vague direction of the hallway.

'Huh. Didn't Frankie leave us anything?'

Frankie was our house manager, accountant, gardener, and cook all in one. He worked at our place four days a week and generally ran the whole family. We needed him because my father was too busy and too important to deal with everyday things, and Helen had just started her articles, so she was busy too. But even before that, ever since my mum left, someone had been here. We had six different nannies before we found Frankie, and they were all hopeless in different ways. Frankie had been with us for four years now, and I for one hoped he stayed forever. Dad and Helen relied on him, too.

Helen made an impatient sound. 'This is Frankie's day off, you might remember, if you took a moment to think. That was why we were going to buy something, right? If you're not happy with sandwiches, perhaps you'd care to get us something. I'm sure I don't mind waiting.' She folded her arms, buttery knife and all, and began to step over to the table.

'Oh, for pity's sake, Helen, we don't need amateur dramatics in the kitchen.'

Helen turned her nose up in an exaggerated look of disdain and returned to her task. 'You should count yourself lucky. Not every old orthopod gets his dinner handmade by an up-and-coming lady lawyer.'

'Not so much of the old, madam!' my father retorted, turning back to me.

I was always, always astonished by the sniping way Helen

and my father spoke to each other. However much it made me squirm, they appeared to enjoy it. Every now and then, they had a total screaming argument, and they seemed to enjoy that too. Both of them were black-belts in the art of the snide remark and the cut-to-the-quick piece of truth you never wanted to hear. My dad, especially, knew exactly which words hurt most. I noticed, though, Helen's clever tactics: her gentle mention of her successful career, and her reminder that as a respected and eminent orthopaedic surgeon, my father ought to behave professionally. Professionalism was a byword with him.

It's not that I didn't love my dad, or that he was a difficult person, or that he didn't love me. I knew for a fact that, in any contest for difficult-ness, I would win hands-down. It was maybe the only thing I'd ever be better at than he was. I was 'reserved, solitary, watchful, and distrustful', according to my school reports. At other times, I knew I could be downright sullen, rude, and obstructive, as my family told me often enough.

Of course, I had perfectly good reasons to be like that, and besides, that was who I was. Mostly.

It didn't help that I actually knew, despite what I mumbled in his direction now and then, that Dad loved me and was always looking out for me. I just didn't always like his way of doing it.

Anyway, while they bemoaned the sad reality of toasted sandwiches for supper—something that suited me fine—I tried my best to imagine an argument that would counteract what I was sure my father would say: that the street cats would be happier and freer if we let them go their own way, that we shouldn't try to impose our ideas of good living on them, that we have no right to interfere, that they are almost feral—and surely not house-trained—and so on and so on. He would say they couldn't live here.

Just like he said ten years previously: 'Your mother can't live with us anymore.'

That time, I never worked out if saying *can't* had meant that she wasn't able to live here, or that she wasn't allowed to. And of course, I never asked.

I pushed that memory aside and tried to concentrate on the search for good reasons why it would be perfectly suitable for Tenner and her kittens to live with us, but I hadn't got far with it when Dad dragged out the heavy wooden chair across from me. He dropped into his seat with all the authority of a principal, folding his hands before him.

'Toby,' he said gravely, 'I want you to tell me everything that happened.'

Helen interrupted. 'Dad! Leave him alone. I already told you everything.'

'I'm not talking to you!' my father snapped. He got cross when Helen tried to get me out of trouble. 'This is important. Let the boy answer for himself, just for once. Tobias! Tell me in your own words.'

I gripped my hands together on the table in front of me. Taking a deep breath, I started at the beginning. 'Helen picked me up after Art. Class was running later than usual, so she didn't have long to wait. It was bucketing rain. We went toward the shops, but then we saw the car in front of us run over a cat. The car drove off, but we stopped to see if we could help.'

For the first time, I looked up. My father was watching me intently. 'Go on.'

I took a deep breath. 'Um, Helen made sure there was a police car to protect us from the traffic. The cat had a broken leg. We said we would take it to the vet.'

My father held up a hand. 'Whoa. You're missing a fair bit of detail right there. Tell me exactly.'

I frowned, trying to remember. 'Helen went to the cat first.

It was on the road, on the driver's side. I followed her, and three kittens jumped out of the verge and pretty much climbed up my leg.'

My father nodded thoughtfully.

At that moment, Helen set a hand on his shoulder and passed over a plate piled high with toasties. I took it from her and put it in the middle of the table. While she grabbed our mugs of tea, I went on. 'The mother cat wouldn't let Helen touch her, so I went to help. She had another kitten in her mouth. I guess she was trying to take them across the road. Anyway, I calmed the cat down, and Helen fixed the break in her leg. We took them all back to the car, and then Tenner told me there was another cat out there in the rain.'

My father held up his hand again. 'The street cat told you?'

'Yup.'

'What did she say? Exactly?'

I thought about it while I took another bite. 'I think she just said "another one", or something like that. I told her she only had four kittens, but she just looked at me. You know.'

Redmond Dartin knew better than anyone. 'I see. Go on. Carefully now, this is the important bit.'

'Well, I walked up and down the verge. It was still showering down. There were no more kittens around, but there was this bracelet. Well, I thought it was a bracelet, with charms, you know, but when I walked past again, it looked more like a bangle. And this one charm on the top, it looked like a cat.'

'Ah. I see. And then?'

'I picked it up. And the charm turned into a cat. Or, well, the charm sort of disappeared, and suddenly there was Katkin.' I nodded in her direction. She quivered at the sound of her name, but didn't rouse from sleep. 'And we came home. All of us. And that's all there is.'

My father nodded.

Helen reached across me for another sandwich. 'Well, Dad? Katkin's a magic cat, then, isn't she? Just like Flax.'

'Not at all like Flax,' my father said solemnly. 'Toby, Katerina has been missing for longer than my lifetime. You've just freed a famous cat from the strongest magic ever known. And I have absolutely no idea how you did it.'

CHAPTER 5
MAGIC

My father had no idea how I released Katkin from the bangle, and I was confused, too. I wasn't even sure that I had released her. I knew I hadn't done anything special. We all talked it through for a few more minutes, in between bites of sandwich, until only a few crumbs were left on the plate. I couldn't come up with a satisfactory answer, no matter how much my father and Helen kept prodding for one. There's no doubt where Helen got the lawyer-ly part of her brain from. They were both really good at pinning me down with just a few words.

'You weren't thinking about magic, you say?' Dad asked.

'Of course, I wasn't.' I tried to stay calm. I hated talking about magic with my father. I'd wished, so many times, that he would stop hoping for me to suddenly sprout magical whatevers.

'You're sure, Tobes? Not even thinking?' Helen put in.

'Not at all, I tell you. I never think about magic. What's the use?' Then, probably because I was saying this for the third or fourth time, a memory came to me. 'Wait.'

'Ah.' My dad sat back with a sigh. 'I've always said there

24

must be some wizardly bone in your body. No son of mine could escape it!'

I threw my father a look, then quickly looked away. *No son of mine.* Honestly! It was like Redmond Felix Dartin thought that every bit of magic in the world was concentrated in him. Just because he chose to use his skills sparingly, and made sure not to put himself into the life-and-death situations that were so challenging for anyone with wizardly talent, he thought that somehow he was morally a better wizard. Rather than torment himself with emergency room crises, for example (where my Uncle Reynard worked), he was an orthopaedic surgeon, concentrating on the precise setting of bones and the fine articulation of joints. My dad specialised in sports injuries, so he hardly ever worked on anyone in a life-threatening situation.

He had explained to me—often—that magic was not a force to be used in conjunction with high emotions. That was how disasters happen, he said. When we were younger, he was always advising us to choose sensible ways to use our magic, to put aside selfish ambitions, and to concentrate on helping our fellow mortals.

Of course, although he still kept an all-too-intrusive eye on me for signs of incipient magic, he stopped offering me career advice a few years ago, when even puberty didn't awaken a single ping of wizardry in me. All he said these days was that I must find something I really wanted to do, some job I could really engage with.

Some job that didn't need any magical talent as a special enhancer.

Only now, I wasn't so sure that something magic hadn't happened. I looked my dad in the eye, a little surprised to find him waiting eagerly while I turned memories over in my head.

'I did,' I confessed. 'Actually, I did think about magic. I said to myself, "Huh, silver plus charm plus cat-shape, and I've looked at it three times—that sounds like magic."'

'Told you so,' Helen muttered.

'And that's when you picked up the bangle?' my father asked.

I nodded. 'Yes. But as I reached for it, the charm thing kind of became Katkin, all at once. I bent down for the bangle, and she jumped into my arms.'

'Oh,' Redmond said, a deep frown appearing between his brows.

I looked at Helen, confused. The searing pinprick of hope that was piercing my heart, the hope that I might actually have some magic in me after all, disappeared when Helen shook her head.

'Don't you see, Tobes? Before you even touched the bangle, it released the cat. That means it was probably Katerina's own magic, not yours, that set her free.'

I dropped my head into my hands.

My father reached across the table to tap my shoulder. 'That's not entirely true, Helen. At least I think not. If Katerina could release herself, why has she been missing for over forty years? Why choose Tobias? No, it's something more complex than that. Let me think.'

Helen and I got to our feet immediately. *Let me think*, in my father's vocabulary, meant *go away and leave me alone a while*.

Helen gave me a hug and headed up to her room, where she had masses of reading to prepare for the next day. I hung around a few minutes, clearing the dishes and stacking the dishwasher, wiping the bench and the table, emptying the teapot, all the while careful not to disturb him. Just as I was about to go to my room and make some kind of effort at my homework, my father flung himself out of the chair and strode into his study.

Probably to ring Uncle Reynard.

Katkin slept on and Flax gave me a down-the-nose look that I read as dismissal. It seemed a good time to check on the street cat family. They were all still nestled in the basket in the hallway. Phew. Part of me was afraid that Tenner would slip out as soon as she had the chance. She was awake and looking goggle-eyed through the open front door. The cold wind was gusting in and the trees in our long front garden threw nightmare shadows across the porch and hallway. I squatted beside the basket, observing that the food bowl was almost as full as I first saw it. However hungry she was, she was clearly saving some for later.

'Tenner,' I said, 'how about I shut that door? There's a little side door you can use if you want to get out, see?' I pointed to the cat flap in the panel by the entry. 'It's never locked. You can come in and out whenever you wish.' As I spoke, I shut out the wind, immediately increasing the temperature in the hallway by entire degrees. 'There! That's better, don't you think?'

Tenner shivered a little and blinked at me. *Is it safe?*

'Of course. Nobody will hurt you here.'

We can stay?

I realised that I hadn't even discussed the little family with my father, but the answer came to me suddenly, in a whole idea. Ha, almost like magic. The street cats could live in the shed where they wouldn't bother Flax. I could use my savings to get them any veterinary attention they needed, and probably de-sexing.

'If you wish,' I told Tenner. 'Tonight you can stay in the house, and tomorrow I'll organise space for you in our shed. It's warm and dry, but no people sleep there. I'll fix the little window so you can get in and out whenever you want.'

Tenner relaxed further into the cat-bed. Her eyes were just

slits now, as if she was almost asleep, or else thinking deeply. *So, we don't have to go home?*

'Oh.' I sat on the floor and rubbed a hand across my face. Tenner had a home. Of course she did. 'Sorry, I didn't know. Of course, you can go home.'

Tenner put back her head and let out a ghoulish yowl. The kittens started meowing, clambering across one another as they tried to cling on to their mother, who had gone all stiff with fear. By the time I managed to calm her down somewhat, she'd climbed half-out of the bed, both front paws clawing deeply into my arm.

'What is it? What's wrong?'

Tenner was not a greatly articulate cat, being very young and completely unaccustomed to sharing her mind with people. Luckily for me, her noise raised both Flax and Katkin, who scratched vigorously at the closed kitchen door to be let into the hall.

Quick! Katkin called.

The only way to get to them was to carry the panicked cat with me. There followed an ungainly and painful scramble as three cats sorted themselves up and down on me, eventually resolving themselves into a huddle on the floor. They all ignored the pitiful noise of the kittens, safely contained in the basket.

Tenner's story emerged in a series of words and images. Somewhere in the middle of this tale, my father arrived to sit beside me on the stairs, looking grim. Mind you, Tenner's story would make any decent being look grim. Katkin sat in front of me and my dad with her tail curled neatly around her and explained it to us, while Flax stayed beside the terrified little street cat, making soothing noises and sending her the message that he would keep her safe from anything and anyone. I could see a new, selfless side of Flax tonight, and I liked it.

I didn't like what Katkin told us.

Tenner's 'home'—if anyone could call it that—was a place where kittens were routinely thrown into rubbish bins or skips, or simply had their skulls smashed, as soon as they became a nuisance or stopped looking cute. Tenner was, as I suspected, the only survivor of her own mother's tenth litter. What I hadn't guessed was that she was the only surviving kitten of all the dozens that her mother had birthed during her miserable life. Tenner's litter mates were dumped in a creek, while her mother was fatally injured trying to prevent it. Tenner was the last remaining kitten, left alone and kept grudgingly to fulfil the role of rat catcher in the overgrown yard and sheds of 'home'.

The story made me feel sick. Katkin, sensing my horror, leaped onto my lap.

There's more, she said. *Having grown up alone with no teaching, Tenner isn't that great at catching rats. When she became pregnant, the 'home' people tossed her out—*

'What do you mean, "tossed" her?'

I mean, they threw her out of their car onto the freeway. She's scratched a living from rubbish ever since, trying to hide from the 'home' people.

No need. They'll never come looking for her, Flax said.

'You're right,' Dad said, entering the conversation.

The real horror of it, though, Katkin said, *is that she's been trying to return there. She and her kittens were starving there on the roadside. Not enough rubbish at this time of year. She thought that at least she would be fed at home.*

Not likely, Flax said, with one eye on Tenner. *We all know how that would have ended.*

'Dad, I already told Tenner she could stay. I thought she might like to have space in the shed.'

'Good idea,' my father said. 'We'll sort it out tomorrow. I've asked Maggie to call around too, to check them over and give us some advice.'

Maggie was our vet and had been as long as I remember. Although she'd never said anything about it, I thought she knew that dealing with any cat in Red Dartin's house would involve certain peculiarities.

I trusted her completely, so I said, 'Do you think she could look at Katkin, too? Just in case, you know, she needs anything. Forty years is a long time to be missing.'

I'm all right. Just so tired.

It's a good idea, Flax put in.

'That's settled, then,' Dad said with a smile. 'What I suggest is that Katkin and Flax keep warm in the kitchen tonight, and we put Tenner's basket in your room, Toby. She and the little ones have quite a bond with you, and you won't mind having your door open this once, I imagine.'

I nodded and then cleared my throat. 'Thanks.'

Dad inclined his head in return and rose to his feet. I noticed that he didn't reach to tousle my hair or pat my shoulder.

'Toby,' he said, 'why don't you get them all settled? Then come to the study, would you? Rain is coming over to talk with you.'

'He is?' Rain is our name for my uncle Reynard. He and my father are twins. 'Red' and 'Rain' to each other.

My father smiled, but there was a certain bleakness to it. 'Yes. We'd better get Helen in too, if she can spare time from her case prep. What's happened tonight is very important. You, Tobias, are about to be the centre of quite a commotion. A magical one at that.'

CHAPTER 6
MAGGIE KHAN

efore Uncle Rain arrived, the front door burst open to reveal Maggie Khan, come to check up on our new livestock. My father asked her to call at her earliest convenience, and so it was no surprise that she made it over in double quick time. For one thing, she was one of my dad's oldest friends—she shared a house with him and Uncle Rain when they were all at university. And she could never resist the lure of meeting new animals.

Maggie was carrying a large cardboard box as well as her hefty medical bag, and looked as energetic and competent as ever. She had her long hair pulled back in a tight plait, and the usual thick black eyeliner emphasising her huge dark eyes. She was quite good-looking in a horsey kind of way—she was tall and slim and had a long, serious face—although Helen once said that Maggie should try to update her look every ten years or so. I quite liked the way she always wore jodhpurs and boots and tailored check shirts. It was kind of dependable.

There was a time when I hoped that my father would marry our vet. That was in the early years after my mother left, when Maggie Khan was the only grown-up woman who was a constant in my life. Teachers, au pairs, nannies, housekeepers, you name it, they always moved on to other positions.

Also, Maggie had a soft spot for my father, which was obvious to me even when I was a six-year-old. At first, of course, I noticed this with fear and loathing and jealousy, thinking that if they got together, then my mother would never return. After a while, though, when the pain of my mother's leaving subsided —or maybe, I should say, was buried a bit deeper—or when I realised that she was never coming back—anyway, a time came when I started to think it wouldn't be a bad idea if he got himself a new partner, and Maggie is by far and away the ...

I was going to say nicest woman of his acquaintance, but she was not really very nice in the way most people think. She was totally no-nonsense, in an absolutely reliable way. I loved the way she said 'Arseholes, Redmond!' whenever she disagreed with my father. She also had a knack of noticing me —*me*—as a separate person. Sometimes that notice took the shape of a very uncomplimentary remark, but at least she always talked to me. I cherished that small hankering for Maggie to live at our house for quite a few years, until one day she visited with her partner, Barb, in tow. They were on their way to the theatre when Dad called her in because Flax had some kind of limp. That was the only time I ever saw her wear a gown. So, I gave up that dream, but I was still always glad to see her.

Maggie stopped still in the hall, her eyes fixed on me as I came downstairs, Katkin in my arms. 'Toby! What's all this about a street cat family? What the—stand still, will you? What have you got there?'

She dumped her gear and grabbed my arm. Katkin, resenting the intrusion, bared her teeth and raised one paw, claws unsheathed. Maggie narrowed her eyes, stepped back, and made a graceful, yielding gesture.

'Oh, my apologies,' she said evenly. 'You're no street cat, are you, little madam?'

Katkin tilted her head, tucking herself more comfortably under my chin. Her claws retracted, but she kept that paw up in front of her face, and two gleaming slits showed that her eyes were still open.

Tobias Felix, she said, *I think I like this one. Feisty. Smart. I like it.* Then she yawned hugely and put her head down again.

I grinned at Maggie. 'No, the street cats are upstairs, but I'd love you to have a look at Katerina too, if you don't mind. Thanks for coming around so quickly.'

By the time Maggie completed her gentle but thorough inspection of all six cats, Dad and Uncle Rain had been talking in the study for quite a while, and we heard Helen go past my door on her way down to them. Even then, Maggie was in no particular hurry, and I appreciated her firm but kind touch as she checked her charges. Katkin agreed to stay in my room, on my bed. Tenner and her kittens nestled in the cat basket on the floor, while we went down to consult with the others.

'Ah, Maggie! Thank you for coming,' my father said, kissing her cheek. 'How are you? How's Barb?'

Uncle Rain made no sign he'd even noticed us. He was seated by the fire with his chin resting on both fists, leaning forward, perched on the edge of a dining chair. Uncle Rain always looked as if he was about to spring into action. Tonight, it seemed he hadn't quite decided what that action would be, but from the look on his face, it would possibly involve fire and destruction.

'Redmond, I've brought you everything you need. The box is in the hall,' Maggie said, wasting no time on chit-chat. 'It's as I expected. As anyone would expect. They're undernourished, full of parasites, filthy dirty, and half-wild. At least it's too cold for them to be jumping with fleas, like most of the undomesticated ones. Mind you, Redmond, these are not feral cats. They're abandoned, if you prefer the word.'

Maggie sniffed. Apparently, the word 'abandoned' wasn't one she favoured herself.

'What's that?' Uncle Rain asked, rousing from his scrutiny of the flames. 'Not feral, but abandoned? How on earth can you tell?'

Maggie rolled her eyes dramatically. 'Good evening to you, too, Reynard. So nice to see you.' She paused one second for a pasted-on polite smile, then got back into preaching stride. 'Feral cats, to answer your question, fear and avoid people, for good reason. Very sensible are feral cats! On the other hand, cats that have been dumped by idiot bastards continue to harbour a stupid belief that humans will help them. These particular cats, according to Toby, approached him. Not the other way around. Ergo, abandoned, not feral.'

'Oh! I see. Haven't met 'em, myself. Yet to get a handle on the whole situation. Just talking the ramifications through with Red.'

'Shut up, Rain,' my father said. 'Anything else I need to know, Maggie?'

Maggie looked at the two men consideringly. 'I smell a conspiracy, you know.' Then she bent to pick up her bag. 'As I said, everything you need is in the box. I'll swing past again on the weekend. Safety, warmth, rest, food, in that order, is what they need. As does the other one.'

'The other one?' my father echoed, frowning.

'Yes,' Maggie said sweetly. 'The one, according to Toby, that you've adopted. The rescue cat that comes from the same private shelter as Flax here. The shelter I've never heard of. That cat.'

'Oh, her. Yes, what about her?'

Maggie cleared her throat ostentatiously. 'Katerina, I

believe, is her name. Well, she's undernourished, dehydrated, and has a healing wound under her armpit, hard to see with such a thick coat, but overall she's in remarkably good shape. Antibiotics for her too. I've marked all the medications.'

'Good,' my father said a bit too boisterously. 'That's good. And, er, for the future?'

'You know the drill, Redmond. I'll neuter them as soon as they're in better shape, when the kittens are old enough. I'm counting on you to pay for that, of course, but mates' rates as ever. Then you'll have to decide what to do with the little family. The mother cat's very young, five or six months old herself, I'd say. Young enough to be adoptable, certainly. After they're fixed, you can take them to that special private shelter of yours. Or to one of the public ones. Or you can register them with the council as your responsibility.'

My father looked at me. 'I'm not sure they'll let us keep six cats.'

'Seven, to be precise,' Maggie said, making her mouth very prim. 'You already have Flax. But if you explain that you're getting them off the streets, making sure they don't breed, and that you're wealthy enough to feed and care for them, you can register yourself as the keeper of a wild cat colony. I'll sign the papers for you, if you like.' Maggie grinned at my father's look of surprise. 'You might house-train them while you think it over. Gotta go.'

She tapped me on the shoulder, and I took her out to the hall again.

'Toby,' she said, 'I'm relying on you to oversee all this. Your father's a good man, but he's not the first one I'd choose when it comes to feeding animals. These cats seem to trust you, and that's rare with these poor half-wild things. They've often been so badly treated beforehand that they never really recover their zest for life.'

Just in time, I stopped myself from telling her all about Tenner's past. After all, how could I possibly know that? So I nodded, thanked her again, closed the door behind her to keep out the cold, and went back to the living room. As I shut that door behind me, Uncle Rain looked up and smiled.

'Tobias,' he said, 'congratulations. You've outstripped your poor old father here, and me too, I daresay.'

I sat down on the couch, frowning at him. 'What do you mean?'

'Well, Red can't even hear that little street cat speaking. Her speech is tiny, infinitesimally tiny. Apparently, you and, er, Katerina, between you, got the whole story of her background. And Katerina herself!' he went on. 'That's brilliant, Toby. She's been missing for decades. She's one of the most important arch-cats. I'm impressed!'

'So am I,' my father said. 'Except that Rain tells me she usually appears in times of great need.'

I looked at his sombre face. 'I'm not sure I understand.'

'He means,' Uncle Rain said, 'that there's every likelihood something is about to go seriously wrong. It might be with the magical world, or the flat one. But something is coming, and it's worrying.'

I understood. The flat world was the one most people inhabited, which just meant they couldn't see the magic. It didn't really matter whether they could see it or not, because magic was all around them in any case. 'Things going wrong' in the flat world meant that ordinary humans were doing stupid, unnatural things that were upsetting the microscopic magical order. 'Things going wrong' in the magic world meant that someone who could see the magic was trying to manipulate it for some (usually selfish) purpose. Either way, it was likely to be bad.

At that moment, I looked around, hoping for reassurance from my sister. But Helen wasn't there.

'Where's Helen?'

'Still upstairs, I imagine. Give her a call, will you, Toby?'

'But I thought I heard her come down when Maggie was here,' I said. I went to check all the same. No Helen.

We looked in every room, in the shed, as far as we could see into the wet and windy garden. No Helen. Her car was still in the driveway where she parked it, with the passenger-side door open. I probably forgot to close it when I picked up Tenner and the kittens. But the car, too, was empty—except for the silver bangle with the cat charm, which lay discarded on the driver's seat.

CHAPTER 7

FRANKIE SAYS

I had a horrible, sick feeling when I saw that bangle on the seat. I knew the bangle was some sort of magic trap, one that held Katkin imprisoned for decades. My imagination went into a frantic spiral, thinking about what that might mean for Helen. My arm was shaking, and I started to point out the bangle to my father and Uncle Rain when I heard them both exclaim at the same time: 'There she is!'

I gasped, suddenly needing some air.

Sure enough, Helen was walking toward us through the rain. She stepped into the porch light at the top of the driveway with her hood up over her head and her phone shining onto the path at her feet.

'Helen!' Dad called, bounding toward her across the slippery paving and into the driving rain. 'Helen! Where have you been? We've been worried sick.'

Helen stood still for his embrace, but after a second, she broke free and moved onto the verandah. 'What do you mean? I told you!' she said, pushing back her hood and tugging off her wellies. The mere sight of her face, with its usual superior expression, released a spring of relief in me. The bangle had burned its shape onto the back of my eye, like a glow of warning that appeared each time I blinked. I thought I'd like Dad and Uncle Rain to have a look at it, so I went to collect it from the car.

It wasn't there.

I covered my little yelp of surprise with a cough and made a show of shutting the passenger door of Helen's car.

'Thanks, Tobes,' she called to me. 'I meant to do that.'

She opened the house door, and we all piled into the hallway, the three of us Dartin menfolk all dripping wet, and Helen looking perfect as ever. She shook her coat a little before she hung it on a peg and turned back to us. Her face lit up with mirth as she looked us over.

'Something the cat dragged in?' she said, then burst into a peal of laughter. 'What is it with you three?'

We continued to stand there, mouths gaping. Her eyes met my father's, and she sobered.

'What, Dad? What's wrong?'

He shook his head dismissively. 'It's all right,' he said in his comforting *don't-worry-I've-got-everything-under-control* voice. 'We couldn't find you. With all that's happened today, I'm afraid I got anxious.' He passed out towels from the hamper under the coat pegs and we dried ourselves off as best we could.

Helen flexed her toes in her thick socks, almost as if she was about to undertake some ballet practice. 'I'm sorry if I worried you, but there was no need. Mia called me for help.' Helen walked into the study and we went thankfully into the warmth.

Mia was our neighbour's daughter, a really nice girl, who was pretty much my best friend. We liked most of the same stuff and usually agreed on things, except that Mia thought of Helen as some sort of goddess and could be really boring on the subject of how perfect and beautiful and talented and knowledgeable and considerate my sister was. Mia was taking Legal

Studies and often asked Helen for help with her homework, and Helen was too kind to say no. Maybe flattered too.

'I popped my head in and told you I was going,' Helen said.

'Well, we didn't hear you,' Uncle Rain noted with disapproval. 'We would have answered if we did.'

'Ha!' said Helen, letting out another burst of laughter. 'Ha! You clearly don't live here.' She gave me a wink and pulled me to sit beside her on the sofa, linking her arm through mine. Her hand was cold, but her voice was warm. 'Lucky to get a nod from your twin, we are. Isn't that right, Tobes?'

My father gave a deep sigh and flapped his hand at Uncle Rain's protests. 'I'm sorry, Helen. I'm a bit unsettled. We couldn't find you, and it's been a very strange evening. It's hard to know what to think.'

Helen shook her head at him reproachfully. 'Dad, did you even ask Flax?'

Dad's mouth dropped open. He closed it with a snap, slapping his palm against his forehead at the same time. 'You're right. I'm being stupid. Stupid! Flax would be the first to sound an alarm if we needed one.' He took a deep breath and let it out noisily. 'Your old father is losing it, I'm afraid,' he said.

'It's just fear,' Uncle Rain said soothingly. 'You're thoroughly scared and full of adrenaline. Bound to make you over-anxious.'

'You didn't think of asking Flax either!' Dad retorted.

'Of course not, Red,' my uncle agreed. 'Flax wouldn't speak to me even if I did.' He reached across to land a soft punch on Dad's shoulder. 'Now I really must go. My shift starts at ten.'

'Yes, all right. And thank you.' My father's voice was gruff. 'You'll come back tomorrow?'

'Day after,' Rain said, holding up one hand like a police officer stopping traffic. 'I'll need some sleep. Toby, Helen, call me if you need me, or if anything, er, happens, okay? Anything Red can't handle alone.'

We sat around for a bit, talking over the day's events and what'd been said, but we didn't make much progress. Our discussion was full of what Katkin's reappearance might mean and what might happen or might not happen, and what might be going wrong with the world of magic or the ordinary world.

Actually, trying to list all the things that might be wrong with the flat world or the magic world would take us all year, and we soon ran out of steam. There were too many possibilities to cover. We changed the topic to the new arrivals.

Helen approved of Maggie's plan for us to adopt the street cats, and she seemed more excited than worried by Uncle Rain's prediction of dire events about to descend on us. 'Imagine if something huge happens! Imagine if we can make a real difference!'

'I've had quite enough imagining for one day,' said Dad. 'Let's leave it for now. I've got a full list tomorrow and I need to clear my head.'

It was too late to start any homework, so I left a note on the kitchen table asking Frankie to wake me as soon as he arrived. I would do it in the morning. I went up to my room, intending to play some music before going to sleep. I planned without Katkin, though, who was sprawled across my bed as though she owned it. She had rested and then occupied herself by organising Tenner and the kittens, explaining and demonstrating the use of the litter-tray, finding and clearing a cosy hiding space for them under my bed, and pulling out one of my school shirts for them to snuggle into.

Apparently, cuddling together against the wall under my bed and on top of my good shirt is, in cat terms, a much better place to be than in the purpose-made cat-bed. As well as making my room pretty stinky, between them they'd created quite an obstacle course from my discarded and overturned belongings.

Just for tonight, Katkin explained. *They're more comfortable with mess. We'll teach them how to be tidy tomorrow.*

'Thanks—I think! Any room for me on that bed?'

Katkin stretched ostentatiously, rolling onto her back. For a small cat, she had quite a reach. I took the opportunity to look her over properly. Her wide green eyes were bright, but she was very thin, and her fur looked dusty and ragged, as though she'd tumbled into a ditch and starved there for days, or maybe weeks. Her tabby stripes were deeply marked and would be striking when she was clean and well fed enough to have a healthy coat. Only one paw was white, all the way up to her left elbow, like she'd stepped into a tin of paint, and she had a neat white bib under her chin. Maggie had shaved off the fur under her left armpit and cleaned an old wound there, leaving a yellow stain of antiseptic fluid on Katkin's bared skin.

All in all, she was the most beautiful cat I'd ever seen.

I thought I'd have bad dreams, given that the bangle image kept appearing in the corner of my eye like an iridescent ringworm, the sort of rainbow image that I got at the start of a migraine. But with Katkin curled across my pillow and the fitful purring of Tenner beneath my bed, I fell into a deep sleep. The next thing I knew, Frankie was tapping on my door, the way he did just before flinging it wide open.

'Good morning, Tobias!' he said brightly, one hand reaching for the curtain pull. 'Nearly seven; time to get up. Goodness, it's smelly in here, time to change those sheets, or put your washing in the basket. Oh, I mean, Frankie says, time to get up!'

This was Frankie's way of getting our cooperation. He never tried to boss us around like other au pairs; he'd always made a game of it, a kind of Simon Says. Though it was years since I'd needed that kind of game, we kept it up as a bit of fun.

When he'd let in the pale daylight to flood the room, he turned to stare at me. It wasn't every day that I had a tabby cat camped out on my pillow, snuggled into my hair, or a chorus of meows coming from under the bed. The stinky litter-tray was a new addition too.

The look on his face made me laugh.

'Morning, Frankie! Thanks, I've got heaps of homework to get through. Rush job, I'm afraid.'

'Uh huh.' Frankie nodded. 'In that case, see you downstairs. My brains are yours to pick.' He was still staring at us.

'Ta.' I stifled another laugh.

'And, er, do we have some extras for breakfast? Friends of our good Flax?'

I sat up, and Katkin draped herself over my shoulder. 'Friends of mine. This is Katkin. Katkin, meet Frankie. And vice versa. And others we can talk about later.'

'Of course,' Frankie said in a soothing voice, but with a twinkle in his eye. 'Others, numbers unspecified, to talk about later. Why not? All that meowing must come from someone. Someones, I should say. Um, how do you do, Katkin?'

I like him, and 'Meow,' said Katkin. *Breakfast?*

'Breakfast?' I echoed aloud.

Frankie gave a theatrical sigh and snapped back into work mode. 'Breakfast, ten minutes. Homework is welcome at the table. Katkin too. Frankie says, get a move on.'

It was Thursday, my father's busiest day in the operating theatre, so he'd left hours before. I found that Helen, too, had gone in early to finish her case prep at work. That meant I had to catch the bus at the end of the street to get to school, which wasn't so bad, because it gave me a chance to do some more reading before class.

Frankie was as good at homework as he was at everything else, cheerfully shelling out clues about probability while he scrambled eggs. He was also very comfortable around cats, which was just as well, considering that he was inundated with a roomful when I came down to the kitchen. Katkin trotted beside me. Tenner followed, carrying Littlest, while I brought Wart and Pink and Footsie in my hands.

'Well!' was all that Frankie said, seeing that Flax greeted them with a fine show of delight, bowing and preening before them. 'This is a surprise, Tobias. Are you setting up a shelter?'

I smiled. 'Almost. We're adopting these ones, anyway. Long story.'

In between maths help and more tea and feeding the mob, Frankie heard all about the car accident and Maggie's visit, and even that Uncle Rain had visited. I didn't say anything about the bangle, though it kept coming into my mind. I finished as quickly as I could and went upstairs again to get ready for the bus.

Where are you going? Katkin asked with an edge in her voice.

'School. I'll be back this afternoon. Will you be okay? Flax is always on guard, and you'll have Tenner and the kittens to mind.'

How many hours?

'I'll be back about 4.30. I'm on the bus today. So, a bit over eight hours, okay?'

Flax leaped to sit beside Katkin on my bed as I put my books into my backpack. I almost fell over with surprise. As far as I can recall, this was the first time he'd ever entered my room. Well, he has the run of the house, so he'd probably been there before, but never at the same time as me. Again, I heard the boom of his voice in my head.

I will watch, Tobias, he said. *We will speak again later. Plans must be made.*

I paused in the act of hefting my bag. 'Do you know more about this? About the problem Dad and Uncle Rain are worried about?'

Flax blinked at me. *We will speak later.*

That was a pretty clear dismissal. 'Fine,' I answered. 'See you later then.'

Be careful, said Flax.

It was probably just the deep throb of his voice that lifted the hairs on the back of my neck, but I shivered as I went downstairs.

CHAPTER 8

A MURDER OF CROWS

The other bonus of catching the bus was that I got to ride with Mia. She was a year younger than I was, but she was such a swot that she was actually in my year level at school. Her being a swot was not such a bad thing, because it meant we could share the bus without ever having to bother about the awkward chit-chat that neighbours waffle on with, like isn't the weather hot/cold/windy/worse than/better than this time last year; what's that thing flowering in your garden; did you see that Chan's corner store have got breakfast cereal on special; isn't it ridiculous how busy the street is getting, there's no parking for visitors; are the McNabs going to sell up or not; what the Lees paid for their new kitchen ... all that kind of pointless blather.

And neither of us ran our life via the school gossip mill, either. I didn't care who went to the movies with Brad Singh, the school hero, or what Bessie Prentice got expelled for. That said, I have to admit that I was interested to learn that Mr Flynn was now engaged to Miss Reibert, but that was only because Helen saw them together at a restaurant she went to with her workmates and got to chatting. That was exactly the sort of thing I could tell Mia, and something we wouldn't bother telling anyone else. Usually we exchanged a sentence or two while we waited for the bus, and once we got on, we both felt free to just get a book out and do something useful.

Today, Mia came running down the street behind me as I headed for the corner stop, shoving her arms through her backpack straps as we said our good mornings. She was always in a hurry because both her parents worked all the time, so it was her job to do the breakfasts and school bags and the getting-dressed-in-proper-school-clothes check and the tooth-cleaning patrol for her four little brothers. There was a baby sister too, but Mia's mum took her to work where they had a kind of crèche thing. One of the aunties came by every morning to drive the boys to primary school. We always knew when that happened because she would beep her horn long and loud until all of them piled into her battered old station wagon. Helen called her Auntie Toot'n'Carmen. Once the boys were on their way to Fern Hills PS, Mia had a chance to get herself ready.

That morning she was looking especially harassed, pushing her hair out of her eyes while she tried to fix her ponytail with one hand and used the other to save her glasses from dropping onto the pavement. I reached out to take the glasses from her and she thanked me as well as she could with a mouth full of hair tie. As I handed them back, I saw a bus coming up behind us. There were heaps of people waiting at the stop, so we would get to the end of the queue in plenty of time, I thought.

Only, just as I turned my head to tell Mia that we would make it, I realised that what I thought was a long line of people in raincoats was actually just a gaggle of scruffy crows. I put my mistake down to the misty weather and sprinted a few yards so I could hold the bus for Mia.

The big, dirty-yellow bus screeched to a halt right at the stop, its doors crashing open so vigorously that water splashed back at me. I scrubbed a hand across my face as I stepped into the stairwell, holding both sides to make sure the door didn't shut before Mia caught up. She was only a step or two behind me, but before I could let her in, a long, uniformed arm reached out from deep in the bus and dragged me fully through the entrance. I shouted a protest, but the bus lurched away from the stop with a roar like a jet engine, and I ended up toppling back into the stairwell. My chin hit the top step and my left arm, trapped by my backpack, was almost wrenched out of its socket. Swearing loudly with all the best words Helen ever taught me, I glared up at the conductor who'd hauled me in.

My mouth dropped open in surprise and every word I ever knew disappeared from my brain.

The conductor looked about seven feet tall and the shape of a weightlifter.

As I continued staring at her, like a wombat in the head-lights, she threw back her head with a laugh. She sounded like she was trying out her voice for a scary killer movie. Then she reached out a huge hand to heave on the straps of my backpack and pulled me to my feet. She pushed her cackling red face down into mine.

'Tobias Felix, honey,' she said. 'Guess who's not going to school today?' And she laughed again. The enormous hand holding onto my shoulder dug deep into my flesh.

On her other wrist, I saw the silver cat-bangle swaying wildly, glinting in the bright lights of the bus.

We sped on.

PART TWO
MIA

CHAPTER 9

THE BUS INCIDENT

THURSDAY

'Stop! Come back here! Toby, stop! Come back!' I yelled and yelled as loud as I could, but the bus sped on.

Then I jumped up and down in the middle of the road, waving my arms absurdly over my head, just like those cheerleader girls from the grammar school.

My backpack crunched against my back as I jumped up, and nearly took my head off as I came down, so I stopped jumping.

I screamed, 'Help! Help! Help!' but there was no one anywhere. No cars, no cyclists, no pedestrians. No one checking their letterbox or bringing their bins in. Nobody going up to the shops or to school or to work or to kinder or to *anything*. Nothing. Nobody.

Okay, okay, Mia Leong Lam, smartest kid in the family, I thought. *What now?*

Breathe, that's the first thing. Right. Breathe. Look around, see what you can see. Remember everything that happened, because you'll have to tell somebody. A part of my brain was screaming, *But there's no one here, you idiot!* I ignored it. Hush, I told myself. Quiet. Think and remember. Get it straight in your head. You're upset. Stop it. Be sensible. You're the most sensible girl in the school; everyone knows that. So breathe. Now think. What just happened?

This is what had happened.

Number one: I missed the bus to school.

On an ordinary day, that would be bad enough, but this was no ordinary day.

Number two: Toby had been so preoccupied with ... something ... that he didn't even razz me about asking Helen for help last night. Usually that would earn me at least one sideways remark about how I was trying too hard and didn't I know Helen had better things to do than to help me with my homework, and maybe one eye-roll or dramatic sigh, but today Toby didn't say anything. He nodded hello and held my glasses like usual while I tied my hair, and did that little thing he always did with the strap that made my backpack sit better, but he wasn't really paying attention. He didn't say, like most mornings when we caught the bus together, 'Haven't your brothers learned to make their own lunches yet?' Maybe he had homework he was thinking through. Or something else. I knew his Uncle Reynard had been there the night before, and sometimes that meant there was some sort of family problem, and if that happened, I never pestered him about it. Toby was a very private person.

Number three: Then suddenly Toby said, 'Here's our bus!' which, really, it couldn't have been, because for one thing, it was two minutes early. Our bus is never early. Usually it's fine to start the long walk to the corner at the time when the bus should arrive. And for another thing, the bus was the wrong colour. But Toby started running for the stop, quick as he could. He went straight through this massive flock of crows doing kamikaze dives onto the footpath all around him. Then this great big mustard-coloured bus screeched to a halt right at his feet, and he grabbed both sides of the door before they even opened properly, getting a face-full of rain off the roof of the bus for his trouble. I called out to wait, that it was the wrong bus, to hang on a minute, and then—

Number four: This weird conductor lady pulled him inside. Her face was all red and blotchy. I saw her clearly as the bus roared away from the stop, its tyres spitting muddy water back at me. She was looking out the rear window, a horrible leer on her face as she laughed at me. She made signs too— slapping her index fingers together like she was telling me off, and great big shooing motions. She even poked her tongue out and wiggled her fingers in her ears, like some unhinged clown.

Number five: Then the bus veered left—not right toward school—and I couldn't see it anymore.

Number six: Yelling and jumping up and down didn't help. There was no one to see or hear.

Number seven: Mia Leong Lam, what you gonna do?

I straightened my backpack and took another deep breath. I needed to tell someone about this. Dad? No, not Dad. He was unreachable at work because he kept his phone solely for jobs coming in. And not Mum if I could help it. My little sister had been really fussy that morning, and I knew Mum would be having quite a time settling her at the work crèche. Aunty Joy? Nope, she was driving the boys to school, and besides, she didn't have a mobile phone because she thought they would fry your brains. Toby's dad? No, it was Thursday, one of his operating days. And Helen had a case on, so she'd have her phone switched off while she prepared. I could phone my school and say—what? That Toby had caught the wrong bus, and I hadn't caught any bus? I could phone 000. Sure. 'What's your emergency?' they would say, and I would say, 'My friend caught the

wrong bus and there was this really mean lady conductor on it.'
Uh huh. Sure.

Then I remembered. Frankie! Thank you, thank you dear universe, for Frankie.

I turned and started running back to Toby's house. Any day that Helen and Mr Dartin were not around at breakfast time, they always got Frankie in. Well, ever since those ridiculous live-in nanny people finished up at the Dartins, the ones who bossed Tobes around after his mum left. We'd just moved in when all that happened. It's how Toby and I got acquainted in the first place. But that wasn't important now. What was important was that Frankie would be there.

Frankie was kind of weird, but really kind. The best sort of help I could get. I really should have thought of him first. My parents used to be a little wary of him, because he dressed really colourfully, for an older guy in his thirties anyway, and then I had to explain to them that he was gay, because they have this thing about making sure I didn't meet the wrong kind of man.

I was fourteen; what did I care about men? They were hairy and smelly, for a start.

Anyway, I had to let them know so they'd stop worrying. To be fair, that was only at the beginning when he was a newcomer in the street, and the home help at the Dartins tended to change pretty often. Once my folks realised that Frankie was staying around and they got to know him, they discovered he was okay. Especially after he had to drive Mum to the hospital when my baby sister Lucky Day (her real name is Lucia Daisy Lam) arrived a week early and Dad was at work, of course, and we were all at school. After that, Frankie and my mum started sharing recipes and shopping tips. And probably gossip too, when no one else was around. So I had no hesitation in dashing up the Dartins' driveway and pummelling their front door as hard as I could.

I'd hardly started when the door swung open so completely that I almost fell into the entry hall. Frankie put out a hand to steady me, shutting out the cold behind us.

'Whoa, what's up, Mia? You missed Toby. He's already gone to the bus stop.'

'No,' I gasped. 'No! Frankie, he got on the wrong bus. Somebody stole him!'

It didn't take as long to explain as I'd feared. Frankie was really quick like that. Before I got to the end of the story, he'd grabbed his coat, phone, and keys. Just as we were heading to his car, the Dartins' cat flew past us and blocked our way. I never realised before just how big he really was. He stood high on all his four paws, his pale ginger coat (that Toby calls 'champagne') literally standing on end. He was a Maine Coon, so really big to start with, and this hair-on-end stunt made him look the size of a Saint Bernard. He was also making one unholy meowing sound.

'Flax, get out of the way,' said Frankie. 'Toby's in trouble, and we're going to help.'

Flax stopped meowing, and his fur subsided so that he looked only the size of a cougar, but he didn't move aside. Frankie made a tutting noise and bent down to lift him away. Flax sat and raised one paw like a feline STOP sign. As Frankie and I looked at one another, wondering what to do next, a smaller cat bounced into the hallway. This one was a neat tabby, a bit on the skinny side, her sides heaving like she'd run from the next suburb. The tabby dashed to touch noses with Flax, then turned and literally sprang into my arms. Before I could work out what to do, she started pawing wildly at the strap of my backpack. I had an idea.

'Is this cat Toby's?'

'Er, yes, I think so,' Frankie answered. 'This is Katkin. She arrived last night with another little cat family they've decided to adopt. I was told they were all pretty feral.'

'That may be,' I agreed, 'but this little cat wants to get into my backpack.'

'Ohhh-kayyyy,' Frankie said slowly. 'Let's make that happen.'

It was the work of moments to unzip the main compartment and dump my books on the hall floor, and a half-second after that, the little tabby was snuggled inside with just her head peeping out the top. I shrugged the backpack into place, aware of the warmth of her little body against me. Flax stepped out of our way as if he had never had a thought of delaying us. In fact, he meowed loudly as if to say 'Get going!'

We went.

CHAPTER 10
THE EMERGENCY DEPARTMENT

Frankie has a tiny car, one of those half-size ones that can park anywhere. It's bright orange so nobody could miss it, even tucked under the big almond tree in the driving rain. The tree was bare of leaves, but I noticed quite a big flock of crows flapping about in its highest branches. There must be some sort of crow convention in town. First, they were all over our bus stop, and now, here at Toby's house. But I didn't have time to give it any further thought as Frankie clicked the lock and I slipped into the passenger seat.

I had to balance my backpack on my knees, which seemed to suit the little cat just fine. She actually snuggled her head in under my chin for a moment, as if to thank me for bringing her along. Then she turned and looked straight ahead, peering through the rain-washed windscreen. Frankie reversed neatly and pointed his car down the Dartins' long driveway. He paused at the gate, looking both ways for any traffic. There was nothing around.

'It's certainly quiet today,' he remarked.

I remembered how deserted the main road had been, too.

'It's like everyone's afraid to get wet,' I said. 'But usually on a rainy day, the traffic is really bad.'

'So it is,' Frankie said thoughtfully as he steered us up to the corner and onto Merri Street. 'I wonder.'

I waited for an explanation of what he was wondering about, but he didn't go on. The cat flicked him one glance, a curious one, I thought, and then returned to her concentrated study of the road. I sat frowning through the swishy wet until we drove up to the bus stop. There was nobody waiting and not a bus in sight.

'Hmm.' Frankie paused only momentarily and then drove on again.

'Where are we going?' I asked. 'I saw the bus turn left up there, onto Darwin Road.'

'I think we need more information before we go chasing it. We're going to the hospital,' Frankie said.

'But Mr Dartin's in surgery all day today! I already thought of that.'

'I know,' he answered. 'But Uncle Rain will be on call at Emergency. He should be easy enough to get hold of.'

I admit that I hadn't thought of that, and that it sounded like a good idea. The hospital is only a few minutes away from our street. As we drove closer, we began to see traffic on the roads. In fact, the whole area was one big jam, and even before we saw all the cars, we heard how the air was filled with the noise of sirens.

At the hospital, there were cars and ambulances haphazardly parked outside Emergency, with others honking their horns and flashing their lights as they tried to drive right up to the entrance. We could see white-uniformed hospital staff milling around the doors, and ambulance officers waving their arms about as they tried to direct people.

'What's going on? It looks like a big emergency. Maybe ...' I didn't know what to say. With things this busy, Toby's uncle wouldn't have time for us, I was sure.

'Maybe is indeed the word,' Frankie said decisively. 'I wonder. Let's see what we can find out here.' He looked across at me. 'Are you bringing Katkin inside?'

'Katkin?' She stared up at me without blinking. 'Yes, I think she wants to come in. She can hide inside my backpack.'

The little cat nodded four times, as if to make sure I saw her.

'Ohhh-kayyy,' Frankie said again. He drove his tiny car over the kerb and to park in the front garden of the hospital, which is just a big eucalyptus tree with some ground covers planted under it, and a wooden bench. I had no idea who would want to sit there, right on the corner of the entry road, but there it was, leaving just enough space to take Frankie's car. Well, there was room if he didn't mind parking on top of the spiky ground covers.

The rain had eased, but huge drips slopped off the gum tree as we got out. One splashed onto Katkin's head as I pulled the zipper nearly closed over her, but she didn't complain. I slung the backpack over one shoulder, cradling it in front of me, and we edged our way through the crowded entry.

Inside the Emergency department, people were gathered in clusters around others sitting or lying on the floor, and staff huddled around patients on gurneys. The place smelled like vomit, with a nasty scent of disinfectant under it all. I wrinkled my nose. It was much too hot in here, and steamy from the wetness of everyone's clothes. I saw slippery blood trails all over the floor, and worse. It looked like a photo of a war zone shown on the evening news, only much more terrible. I couldn't imagine what disaster could possibly have caused all this.

Frankie stood still for a moment, scanning the room. Then he turned and looked down at me, his face pale. 'This way, Mia,' he said. 'I'm afraid this is bigger than we thought.'

He led the way toward the reception desk, but I didn't think we could get very close because of the crowd. I kept right behind him, one hand cradling the backpack so Katkin wouldn't be jostled or frightened. As we wended our way through, I heard snatches of what people were saying:

That crazy bus! Must have been driven by a maniac! Drove straight at us.

Bounced off the traffic light right onto the footpath!

Took my side door right off!

Never stopped once!

Drove right at that pedestrian!

'Frankie!' I hissed. 'It's the bus. It must be the same bus.'

'I heard,' he said over his shoulder. 'This way.'

I followed him to the reception desk, which was as chaotic as tuck-shop at morning recess, with just as much shouting and pushing, and horrible crying and screaming too. A harassed-looking nurse was trying to get people to speak one at a time, but he was fighting a losing battle. Beside him, an ambulance officer appeared to be in charge of everything. She directed gurneys into cubicles, and pushed—and I mean actually pushed—nursing staff toward particular tangles of people, all the time talking non-stop into her comms unit like she was a commentator at a big event. As we approached, she put a finger over the microphone.

'Do you have injured with you, sir?'

'No,' said Frankie, 'but we need to see Professor Dartin, right now. We have information about this disaster.'

The ambulance officer waved another gurney past and took hold of an IV drip for a moment, while a nurse fiddled with the line. That done, she looked us over.

'Information? Maybe the police, hey? Sorry, but you need to get out of our way.'

'But ...'

'Sorry,' the ambulance officer said again. 'Not now. We're kind of busy, for Pete's sake. Hey! Not so fast, that's a neck injury on that gurney!'

We had lost the attention of the one person who seemed clear enough to listen to us. I pulled on Frankie's arm and he bent down to hear me.

'Maybe we should go,' I said. 'We can't get to Uncle Rain, and this place is making me feel sick.'

'Wait,' he said. 'Don't throw up just yet.' Then he yelled above the racket in the room. 'Professor Dartin! Reynard! Over here!'

I couldn't see past the press of people, but I was suddenly bumped aside as Toby's Uncle Rain appeared, his gloved hands held up, his crooked elbows giving him a bit of space in the crush.

'Frankie! What is it? Someone hurt? Not Toby?'

Frankie leaned in close and muttered in Professor Dartin's ear.

'Oh, my word!' said the professor. 'It's her again; it must be. Poor Toby.' He glanced around distractedly, as if he didn't quite know what to do next. Then he looked down at me, and back at Frankie, and seemed to steady a bit.

'Right,' he said. 'I can't come now, but I'll get a message to Red. You can see the damage. I'm sure the police are already on her trail, but ...'

'You'd like us to see what we can find out. We'll do our best,' said Frankie.

'I'm so sorry,' said the professor. He turned to me. 'And you —Mia, isn't it? I'm sorry for you too. Maybe Frankie can take you home first.'

I was about to protest when a nurse grabbed the professor's arm and dragged him away. He left with a backward look, lifting his eyebrows to us as he returned to the disaster victims in the waiting area.

Frankie found a way outside again. Weak rays of sun were now ripping tiny wisps of steam off the paved roadway and glinting off the wet vehicles still jammed in the Emergency area, making me squint against the glare. Frankie led the way back to the car. He'd forgotten to lock it, so we had to wait while he clicked lock-open-lock-open, and then we got in. I pulled my backpack onto my knees again, and Katkin pushed her head out.

'Meow,' she said, sounding like a question. I translated what I thought she meant.

'What now?' I asked. 'What can we do?'

Frankie started the car. 'A lot,' he said, reversing carefully over the kerb. 'First things first. Do you still feel sick?'

'No, I'm fine,' I answered.

'Do you want me to drop you at home?'

'No way!'

'Good,' he said, picking his way through the badly parked cars and avoiding the press of vehicles still trying to get close to the Emergency entrance. 'What we do now is go find Toby.'

Katkin made a loud meow, something like approval or eagerness.

I took a deep breath. 'We're going after the bus?'

'We are. I think I know where she might be headed.'

'She?' Professor Dartin's words came back to me. *It's her again, isn't it?* he had said. 'Frankie, do you know what's happening?'

'I have an idea. First, let's find that bus.'

'Sounds good,' I said, and Katkin agreed in a half-growl. 'But first I think you'd better tell me everything you know.'

CHAPTER 11

WHAT FRANKIE KNEW

We drove back toward Darwin Road. As we came close to the traffic lights, they morphed into orange, then red, and Frankie pulled up, clicking his tongue with impatience. As soon as the car came to a complete halt, a large crow landed on the tiny bonnet.

'What the ... what?' said Frankie. 'Get off, you mangy creature! Get off my car!' He flapped his hands at the windscreen, but the big bird took no notice. It just mantled its wings extra wide and let out an ear-splitting screech.

'It's another crow,' I told him over the noise. 'About the hundredth I've seen today. A whole flock of them was at the bus stop, and then there was another lot of them in Toby's almond tree. Didn't you see them before?'

Frankie looked at me sideways. 'Crows? Really?' The light changed to green, and the crow leapt away, flying quite low where we could see it for a while, until it lifted high over the traffic ahead of us and disappeared from view.

'All right, that was odd,' Frankie said thoughtfully. He shrugged his shoulders and wriggled his body, as if his fancy jumper was somehow itching him. 'And you've seen more of them today?'

'Earlier today, yes. They were there when Toby got on that bus, and they were in the Dartins' garden.'

'I wonder,' said Frankie.

I let out a noisy breath. 'You've said that three times already! What is it that you wonder?'

Frankie turned onto Anzac Street, a smaller road leading east, away from school and home and town. 'Three times, have I? What are you, Mia, the world's countingest girl? Crows and crows and every word I say ...'

'*Meow!*' Katkin said really loudly, before I could even start to tell Frankie what I thought of his grown-up delaying tactics. The little cat batted at his hand on the steering wheel. '*Meow!*' she said again.

'Pull over!' I ordered, feeling that the cat had told me to take charge right at that moment. 'Before we go any further, Frankie, you'd better tell me what you think is going on. You keep hinting and nodding to yourself. If we're going after Toby, you'd better tell me everything. There's no point in me being here if I'm in the dark, and it would just waste time to take me home. So stop right here and speak!'

'*Meow!*' said Katkin, nodding repeatedly.

'And Katkin wants to know what you know, too! So tell us everything. Now.'

'Oh-kay,' Frankie said in quite a nice voice, considering that Katkin and I were so cross with him. 'Here we go then. The get-Toby-back planning meeting is about to begin.'

He pulled his little orange car into a spot outside the RSL, which was closed at this time of the morning. Katkin inched herself higher in the backpack, and with an impatient little sigh, pushed her way completely out of the bag and onto my knee. She leaned against me, her head tucked under my chin, her little face pointed directly at our annoying driver.

Frankie may have been talking light-heartedly, but he looked genuinely worried, his face relaxing into a scowl as though his previous composure had been just an act to keep me calm. He cocked his head at us both.

'Mia, what do you know about Toby? About Toby's mum, in particular?'

I felt Katkin's head turn against my throat as she looked up at me. This was a difficult topic, and it gave me a strange feeling to think that Toby's mum was mixed up with his kidnapping. Surely she wasn't that obnoxious bus conductor, grabbing him back from that nice Mr Dartin? I took a deep breath.

'Well, when we moved in next door, she'd only just gone. It was pretty messy, from what I know. Toby couldn't really talk about it, or wouldn't. He was too upset. He just told me she was gone and was never coming back.'

'Hmm,' said Frankie. 'Did he say anything else?'

This conversation wasn't going as I thought it should. I wasn't the one holding back information. We should at least trade questions.

'Hang on a minute, Frankie. How come you get to ask so many questions? You're meant to be telling me things, not the other way around, if you don't mind.'

'I will, I will. I will tell all, I promise. I just want to know where to start. You see, even what you've said so far tells me that you've known Toby longer than I have. You might remember something that helps. Please.'

'Meow,' Katkin said almost in a purr, as if to agree. She patted my chin with a soft paw, claws well-sheathed.

'All right,' I said. 'We'd only just met, down in the back garden—you know all the gardens in our street are really long, right, except the ones where there's a new house built in the back? So, there's this section right down in the back garden where the shrubs along the side don't quite make a fence. A gap in the hedge. We can use it like a crossing so we can get through without going all the way round to each other's front door.'

'I've never noticed that!' said Frankie.

'It's easy to miss. I can show you. It's something only Toby and I know, and we don't use it much anymore. When we were young, though, we used it all the time.'

'I see.' Frankie, bless him, didn't say anything about us still being young, which is what my parents would have done. I went on.

'Well, he was really sad about his mum going, and then it got worse.'

'Worse? How so?'

'The Dartins hired these stupid live-in nanny people; like, there were about five of them, one after the other. Before you came, you know. They were hopeless, and bossy, and one even tried to change Toby's room around, which was crazy, because anyone with eyes in their head can tell that he wants to leave it just the way his mum made it for him.'

'Yes, indeed,' said Frankie. 'How extraordinary. Even I know he doesn't want anything changed. I didn't know why, though. Thank you.'

I frowned at him. He seemed genuine, so I continued my story. 'Well, he loved his mum.'

'He's not cross with her for leaving him?'

'Of course not! It wasn't her fault, he told me. Mr Dartin wouldn't let her stay.'

Frankie almost jumped out of his seat with surprise. His eyes opened as wide as they could go, and it took him a few seconds to close his mouth.

'What? Oh my goodness, what a mess! How could he possibly think that?'

I shrugged. 'Because he said she couldn't live with them anymore. Toby's dad said it, I mean. Like she wasn't allowed to.'

'I see. Good grief,' Frankie said, pressing both hands against his mouth for a moment. Then he shook himself a bit and pressed the ignition button. 'Mia, do you mind if we start driving again? I'll tell you what I know, I promise you. Sincerely. But we need to move on.'

This sounded like a good idea. I buckled up, and Katkin stayed on my knee. I pushed the backpack to the floor. As the car headed out onto the road, Frankie made some odd noises, whistling through his teeth and clicking his tongue.

'Where to start?' he muttered. 'Oh well, in for a penny, in for a pound, and you are such a nice girl. Nice girls, I should say,' he amended, as Katkin swiped at his hand on the wheel.

'Mia, how much do you know about magic?'

CHAPTER 12

WHAT MAGIC REALLY IS

'What do you mean?' I asked cautiously. 'No, don't answer that. I have an open mind, all right? Now just tell me what it is you have to say.'

Frankie checked the rear vision mirror and peered through the windows, looking for any hazards, or maybe for crows. It was quiet here on Anzac Street. I thought that perhaps everyone was over at the hospital, or stuck at the scene where the bus had run into those people. I could still hear sirens, but the sound was growing fainter as we drove away. A helicopter passed over us, heading back toward the city.

Frankie slowed briefly as we drove past a primary school—it was still early enough for speed restrictions—and then sped up after we turned right at the T intersection of Anzac Street and Boundary Road. This was the way up to the hills; I knew from the times we went there for picnics. Frankie seemed sure about where he was going, so I just held Katkin in close and waited for him to talk.

Eventually he said, 'Well, Mia, you know Toby, and you know the Dartins, so you realise they're not an ordinary family.'

'Mmm.' I could have asked him to define what he meant by 'ordinary family', but I didn't want to interrupt him.

'They, er, they belong to the, er, the world of magic.'

'Magic. I see.'

'I don't expect you do,' said Frankie. 'Mia, I grew up in a magic family, but I'm flat. That means, I can't do it myself. I can't see magic or hear it, although I know it's there. It's a bit like being born colour-blind. You know there are such things as colours, and you can tell the difference between most of them, and you just have to believe everyone else when they go into raptures about how wonderful and brilliant those colours are. Are you following?'

'Sure. Are we going all the way to the reservoir?' He had turned onto the Mountain Highway, which is quite a fancy name for what is just a narrow, winding road.

'Possibly. Do you want me to go on?'

Katkin went 'Meow!' and I said 'Yes!' at the same time. Frankie smiled.

'All right, ladies! Now, most of us live in the flat world. We can't see the magic. It's like—hmm, do you know about chaos theory?'

I nodded. 'Yes. We talked about that in maths. It's a theory that shows how great big changes can start with very small events.'

'That's right. Butterflies wiggling their antennae can cause typhoons—that's a very unfair summary, but you've got the idea. Okay, so people who can see magic can see the relationship between tiny events and enormous consequences.'

'Wow.' I thought about that for a while. My mother sometimes warned my little brothers not to play too roughly, or someone would lose an eye. It had never happened that I knew of, and I always thought she just loved exaggerating everything. Although maybe she had some sort of hint about the magic world—that events could start out quite small and later get out of hand. Maybe, I thought, but probably she just wanted them to quiet down, and it had nothing to do with chaos theory or magic. Maybe it was just the way of the flat world too, that little events snowballed into bigger ones. Maybe the magic world and the flat world were pretty much one and the same.

Thinking that made me say to Frankie, 'So magic isn't real? It's just things that happen? Just nature? Little actions and giant results, but all in the natural way of things?'

'Oh, magic is real all right,' said Frankie. 'But in a way, you're right. Magic is quite normal and very much part of the natural world. It's not mumbo-jumbo and long robes with stars all over them and spooky spells and old curses. That's just window-dressing and make-believe. But the chaos theory example is only part of it. It's much more complicated than that, but so is everything else in nature. Humans only know the half of it, but we're learning all the time. Let me think. Ah, that might work. Have you ever heard of spontaneous generation?'

'Spontaneous what?'

Frankie nodded a bit too enthusiastically, quite as if he expected that I would never have met this particular theory in Year 10 Science. 'So, back in very ancient times, people started studying the natural world in a kind of scientific way. Aristotle is a good example; you've no doubt heard of him.'

'I don't think so.'

'Really? Oh. Well, he was an early Greek philosopher. The classics. No?'

'Just go on, okay?'

'Sure. Early scientists tried to discover things by doing experiments, just like we do today. One of the experiments was about how life begins.'

'How did they experiment with that?' Katkin pushed her

head under my chin. She was almost purring, as if she found Frankie's explanations quite funny.

'Well, ancient thinkers didn't have microscopes and petri dishes and infrared, so they kind of just watched the natural world. I think I heard about one where someone put a lid on a clean glass jar and *voila!* Within a few days, there was all kinds of mould and insects in there.'

Katkin did her little funny purr again, leaning back against me. She seemed much amused by the idea.

'Of course!' I said. 'I bet the jar wasn't sterilised properly. Germs and bacteria and fungus and tiny eggs.'

'That's it exactly. They couldn't see all the micro thingies, so they decided that the live material had spontaneously gener-ated. As in, life had just started all by itself, in a closed glass jar.'

I thought over what he had said and decided that it made good sense. 'Easy enough mistake to make, I suppose. Hygiene wasn't good then, either.'

Katkin nodded vigorously, as if she knew all about hygiene practices in Aristotle's time.

'But what does that have to do with magic?'

'Oh, nothing,' Frankie said annoyingly. 'Nothing at all. It's just a way of explaining that simply because we don't under-stand magic, it doesn't have to be, um, magic—it could just be perfectly natural, only we don't have the means to explore or understand it.'

I think he said a bit more, but I'd stopped listening. I couldn't get my head completely around magic, but that wasn't what was worrying me. I looked through the rain-streaked car window at the wet trees and dripping ferns that lined the road. I was waiting for Frankie to get to the point. The bit about Toby's mum. I really hoped to the deepest part of my heart that she wasn't the red-faced, scary-looking lady who had stolen him.

Katkin's claws suddenly dug hard into my thighs, and she made an almighty yowl. We had driven around a tight bend, and in front of us was the back half of the ugly yellow bus.

Its front end was dangling over the sheer drop above the reservoir.

Frankie's car skidded to a halt. For a long moment we just sat, open-mouthed, staring at the scene in front of us, while Katkin continued her unearthly caterwauling. A dense flock of crows circled the wreck like a small tornado, cawing and screaming as they flung themselves round and round in a riot of feathers and noise.

'Oh no!' said Frankie, throwing his door open wide. He leapt from the car. I pushed at the handle on my side and followed, Katkin springing off my lap and racing toward the stricken bus.

As I went after them, kind of wringing my hands and saying stupid things ('Oh! Oh! Oh!'), I heard another car brake behind us with a loud shriek. I looked over my shoulder and saw Dr Khan, the vet, jumping from her 4WD.

Her eyes were open so wide that her black eyeliner looked like holes in a mask. She wasn't making any more sense than I was. 'Oh no!' she kept saying.

All the same, I was grateful when she came with me across the road to stand beside Frankie.

He was peering into the bus, one hand on either edge of the doorway as he leant forward to see in. Most of the bus was already hanging over the precipice. He took a step back, nearly treading on Katkin, who was rocking beside him, still crying her piercing cat refrain.

Frankie looked at us, shaking his head. 'Empty,' he said. 'There's no one inside.'

PART THREE
TOBY

CHAPTER 13

WHAT HATE LOOKS LIKE

The scary conductor cackled again as she shoved me toward the back of the bus. I scrambled away from her as well as I could and climbed into a seat. She leaned into the back window and made a concert of rude gestures at Mia, who was jumping up and down in the middle of the road. Then the bus flung itself around a corner, going left instead of right toward school, and I hung on tight as it suddenly gained speed.

The big woman lurched back up the central aisle. As she went past me, I shrank against the window.

'Quickly, you moron!' she screamed at the hunched driver, who was braking as we approached a red light. 'Keep driving! Keep going!' She thumped his back viciously until the bus regained speed.

I braced myself just in time as we sideswiped a delivery van and kept going. Pedestrians scattered out of the way. We powered through an intersection and I couldn't stay quiet any longer.

I started yelling, 'Stop! Stop! What are you doing? This is completely wrong. Stop!'

Neither of them took a bit of notice. The driver made a kind of coughing noise, and I saw then that his hands were furry and clawed on the wheel. I was glad I couldn't see his face.

Its face.

Ugh.

What could I do? I pressed the red button to light up the 'Next Stop' notification, but that made no difference. These two had gone completely rogue, and this was insanely dangerous.

Just as I had that thought, the bus smashed into the back of a stationary car at a pedestrian crossing, pushing it into the path of a gaggle of schoolchildren and mums. I couldn't see if anyone had been hit.

The impact threw me off my feet, but straight away, the bus backed up and then charged around the mayhem. I could hear screams and wails behind us, cars tooting their horns, and people yelling. Our bus just kept going.

Right. This was just too stupid, magic or no magic. I didn't care that the weird conductor was wearing the enchanted bangle, or that the driver was some spelled-up rodent creature out of hell. This bus had to stop. People were being injured, maybe killed. I shrugged out of my backpack and stumbled toward the front of the bus. The conductor blocked my way to the driver. I reached up to grab her by the shoulders.

'Stop this! You are being really stupid. Stop this bus, now!'

She laughed as she punched me.

I was thrown backward and my head hit the floor, hard. I only just saved myself from falling down into the stairwell by catching hold of a seat leg. The huge woman exploded with rage and kicked me all over until the only place I could retreat to was on the lowest of the stairs.

'Shut up!' she screamed at me. 'Shut your stupid mouth! Your bloody mother's son is what you are, and the more you behave like her, the worse it's gonna be for you. You hear me, moron? I'm gonna get her back, right? I'm gonna get her back good!'

She kicked me again, aiming for the side of my face and collecting my shoulder on the way. I tucked myself away from her. Two thoughts ricocheted inside my head: this was about my mother, and this was what hate looks like. This strange woman wanted revenge on my mum. It made no sense to me.

I stayed in my protective crouch while I decided what to do. The first priority, I thought, was to get this stupid killer bus off the road before anyone else got hurt. I tried not to think about what had happened behind us, but to concentrate on making sure that it didn't happen again.

I lifted my head cautiously from behind my arms, but Revenge Woman wasn't watching me now. She was up the front again, smacking the driver round the ears and pointing up the hill. I saw that we'd left town and were heading for the lookout. Well, no more traffic lights at intersections, and no more pedestrian crossings. That was good.

But ...

There was a kindergarten up this road, and at this time of the morning, the same parents-dropping-off-kids scenario that we saw at the local schools would be playing out. Yes, on a narrower road, with lots of slow-moving pushers and prams, and dawdling toddlers and distracted mums. My only option was to stop the bus.

It was more difficult than I expected. I mean, I did okay crawling from my hidey-hole and along the aisle until I was just behind Revenge Woman, but then I kind of froze. It's not an easy thing to do. Nobody really wants to deliberately crash their vehicle over the side of a mountain. But that's what I did.

I surged up from the floor, catching the conductor by surprise as I shouldered her aside. I snatched at the steering wheel and wrenched it all the way right. On a road that narrow, that millisecond's loss of control was enough to send us ploughing through the barrier. The bus now hung over the void, the driver's frantic lunge for the brake pedal making the back tyres squeal as they skidded across the asphalt in a rubbery arc.

I got to my feet quicker than the other two and ran to the back of the bus. I smashed the emergency window and scrambled through it and onto the road. As I looked about to see which way to run, a massive kangaroo-rat scuttled past me, headed into the bush by the side of the road.

That got rid of the driver.

I turned back toward town and began to jog downhill. Just then, a huge, taloned hand grabbed my arm.

'Not so fast, little man,' Revenge Woman said. 'You're coming with me.' She hauled me along the edge of the cliff, dragging me uphill until she reached a gravelled bike track leading around the side of the mountain toward the waterfall.

I cartwheeled my arms and kicked at her, but she was amazingly strong. She was fast too, towing me along with her as if I weighed nothing, her clenched hand like a vice on my arm. I could hardly stay on my feet, and even though I did everything I could think of to break away from her, she just hung on. I clutched at the railings along the edge, but I couldn't hold my grip. She just thumped my hand away and kept going. I leaped up to catch at tree branches, but that didn't work either. I fell onto to my knees trying to hook my arm around a tree, and that didn't even slow her the tiniest bit. Revenge Woman was like an old-fashioned steam engine, puffing and gasping with effort as she tugged a load up the hill, but not once slowing or stopping. Great name for a famous train, I thought. All aboard the *Revenge Woman*, for the trip of a lifetime to the top of the mountain.

In just a few minutes, we got as high as the terraced lookout next to the waterfall. Here she twisted her other hand into the collar of my jacket and shoved me into the little wooden hut near the edge of the path, slamming me onto the ground so hard that my face hit the dirt floor. The hut was where tourists stood to get good photos of the white rush of water tumbling down the rock wall, and also where they could stand away from the waterfall's spray. The hut was tiny and dark and cold, and a little smelly. Not the sort of place you'd want to be trapped inside with a bully.

Revenge Woman put her enormous hands on her huge hips so her bulk blocked the entire open side of the hut, even dimming the splashy roar of the waterfall. I got to my feet and shook myself into some sort of order, pointedly ignoring the tirade of swear words belching from her twisted mouth.

'I think I've had enough of your company,' I said, doing my best impersonation of my father at his most annoyed. I ostentatiously straightened the cuffs of my shirt under my school jacket. My nose was bleeding, so I blotted it on my sleeve, pretending that this was something I did as a matter of course and really too far beneath my dignity to notice. I looked at Revenge Woman, who had her eyebrows lifted in surprise at my attitude. A little less certainly, I went on. 'You are angry and rude and violent, and I don't want to spend any more time with you.'

She laughed, and this time it seemed in genuine amusement. 'Angry and rude and violent,' she said. 'And that's not all, little man. I'm also magic!'

She did a strange thing with her arms, as if she was an olden-time aircraft operator, guiding some enormous plane onto the tarmac with paddles and exaggerated aerobatics. She finished with a spectacular yoga tree stance and beamed at me, one foot braced against the opposite knee, her hands in a prayer pose over her heart. Her wide mouth was full of large yellowing teeth, so her smile wasn't very reassuring. I didn't look too closely, because the smell of her breath convinced me that she never ate anything but stale garlic. Apart from that, nothing happened.

'Not as magic as you think, it seems,' I said.

Revenge Woman laughed again, a really ugly sound. Actually, it was a very over-acted sound, like an amateur putting on a weak Joker impression.

I shook my head. 'Please. Let's stop these dramatics.'

She spread her arms wide, still grinning. It was then I noticed that the waterfall, the trail, and the bush—in fact, everything outside the hut—had vanished. We appeared to be drifting in the middle of a formless cloud, cocooned inside a small and smelly timber building.

'Oh.'

Revenge Woman smirked.

I tried to keep my father's calm demeanour. It was either that or start screaming with fear. I sat down cautiously on the hard, wooden bench that lined the hut's back wall, hanging on tight to hide my shaking.

'Well, seeing as we have some privacy now,' I said, 'why don't you tell me what this is all about?'

CHAPTER 14

THE WORST EXAM OF MY LIFE

My father often told me not to worry so much, especially about exams.

I was the kind of kid that got into a huge panic in the days leading up to any test. I would be quiet, but inside I was panicking. I wouldn't sleep at night and I would lose interest in food. I'd have horrible dreams where I always turned out to be a complete fraud. I once dreamed that Mr Flynn opened up my head as I was writing my answers, and discovered that I was actually a stuffed toy filled with jellybeans instead of real brains.

I had that same anxious feeling as I sat on the hard wooden bench, waiting for Revenge Woman to respond. My heart was bouncing around my chest like a ping-pong ball and my thoughts were careering all over my head, tearing great gouges through my brain. My mother, the carnage, the bus, Mia, the kangaroo-rat-driver, magic, the cat-bangle that Revenge Woman was wearing—all these images flashed across my mind like strobe lighting.

I wished Helen was with me. She always knew what to do.

Then I snatched the thought back. I didn't want anyone else in this trouble.

I straightened my shoulders. Now was the time to harness the adrenaline that rushed through me. This was much worse than the worst exam of my life, but even so, surely my usual strategies would do some good. Anything was better than the shivering helplessness that threatened to overcome me. *Act. Think fast, write fast*—or in this case, *talk fast.*

Revenge Woman was still staring at me, her face rather like the ferocious mask on the cover of *Medea* that we studied last year. Behind her, the magical fog she'd made billowed and swirled, like the air was breathing in and out. I ignored the nauseous feeling it gave me and repeated my question.

'Really, I think I deserve to know what's going on. Do you have a reason for bringing me here? Something so important that you don't care whether we ran anyone down with that insane bus? And perhaps you might tell me why you keep mentioning my mother?'

At each question, her face grew even less amused, but also less threatening in a strange way. Her presence somehow diminished as she blinked at my words. Then she folded her thick arms across her wide chest, making a visible effort to keep her anger hot.

'What makes you think I'm interested in your questions, little man?' She glared at me. 'You are nothing more than an ant, are you? You may as well be a total flat, you stupid useless boy. You don't deserve even a minute of my time. I don't have to answer questions from flats or children. Certainly not from a stupid flat child. So just shut up!'

I thought of several smart answers to that, such as, if she didn't want to waste time on me, I was more than happy to leave, but I didn't see how that could work while she had us magicked up into a cloud. So I tried again to get her to talk to me.

'You're right, of course,' I said, keeping my voice even and low, pretending that she hadn't been bellowing at me. I looked at a button sewn onto the collar of her uniform. It was easier than looking at her face. 'Whatever it is you're after, I'm afraid you've got yourself a pretty hopeless bargaining chip. I'm no use to you at all. I have no idea who you are or what you want, and even if I did, there's no way I would help you get whatever it is that you're trying to get.'

At my first words, Revenge Woman unfolded her arms and took a step toward me. She had her fists clenched, and I was pretty sure I was about to get my face smashed in again. Then she stopped, staring at me as I finished what I was saying, so I just went on in the same voice. As my pretty speech ground to a halt, she shook both fists at me.

'What do you mean, you don't know who I am?' she growled. 'Who the hell else would I be? I'm Orsa, you idiot boy. Orrrr-sssss-aaa!'

She was furious, but so confused and shaken that even though she was shouting louder than ever, I started to feel much less afraid. The hairs on the back of my neck slicked down again, and I paused to calm myself with a count of five. Then I crossed my arms and leaned against the hut wall.

'I'm so sorry,' I said in mock sincerity. 'I've never heard of you. Orsa, you say? Should I know you?'

'Should you ...' She sat down with a loud thump on the bench across from me.

Through the now empty doorway, I could see that the clouds of her magic were spinning wildly, with strands of violet and yellow threading manic pathways through the vapour. I looked back at Revenge Woman. Orsa, I should say. She was crumpled down to half the menacing size she had been, as if she were a huge balloon with the air let out. She wasn't even as high as my shoulder now.

I met her eyes curiously. 'Orsa, that's your name? Orsa, what is it I should know?'

She waved a hand at me. 'Shut up,' she muttered. 'I'm thinking.'

Well, that was better than beating up on me, but I was pretty worried about the violently swirling turbulence that was brewing inside the cloud she'd made. I tilted my head at it, once again copying my father's actions, and narrowed my eyes. Surely a magic cloud of that density would react to all sorts of influences, maybe even one as feeble as mine.

Calm, I thought at it. *Time to settle into a nice, calm cloud. Nothing is really wrong. We're actually still sitting in a dear little hut on the side of the waterfall trail, and you are a beautiful cloud of mist and serenity. No one is in danger, and the whole of nature loves you.*

I thought on for a bit more like that, and perhaps the cloud settled. The most lurid of the purples and yellows faded into pastel shades, and the swirling slowed. Of course, it was probably reacting to Orsa's mind rather than mine, but it made me feel a lot better to see that a tiny thread of normality was returning to the scene.

I hoped that the cloud would disappear completely and that I'd see the trail, but it stayed put. Oh well. Better get her talking again. The more time she spent talking, the more time for someone to come and find us. A bus hanging over the edge of the mountain road would be noticed pretty soon. And Mia— Mia wouldn't give up on me. She wasn't the kind of friend who'd shrug her shoulders and find some other way to get to school. She'd come after me, or find someone who could. Time, that was all I needed, time when Orsa wasn't thumping me, or taking me farther away from home.

'Orsa?' I said gently. 'Is there anything you want to tell me? Anything you need to explain?'

To my surprise, she put her head in both hands and groaned.

'There, there,' I said automatically, and then stopped myself. I didn't really care if she felt bad or useless or terrified or sick. The sooner I could hand her over to some responsible authority, the better for everyone.

'Shut your face, flat boy,' Orsa muttered, looking up. 'No one's gonna hand me over to any authorities ever again.'

Oh. Great. Had I said that aloud, or was she reading my mind?

Orsa laughed at my consternation. 'Isn't that what you were thinking? It doesn't take a genius, you know, to read faces. It doesn't even need magic. Even you could learn it, flat boy.'

I shrugged. 'Well, you have to admit, your behaviour is kind of strange. You kidnapped me, and drove your bus like a maniac through people and cars. Of course the authorities will want you.' She turned her face away from me, arms crossed, as if pretending that she couldn't hear me. Then a thought struck me.

'Hold on a minute, what do you mean, "ever again"? Orsa, have you escaped from somewhere?'

CHAPTER 15

HER BIZARRE ANSWER

That was the only thing I could think of, even though it felt like the plot of a dud movie. What if Orsa had escaped from some sort of facility, you know, where they kept people who were a danger to themselves and society? Maybe she'd escaped from prison. There was no other reason for her to say that no one would hand her over to the authorities *ever again*, unless someone had already done it in the past.

I didn't know much about such places, but she was acting like a character in a low-budget horror movie, and she certainly deserved to be locked up for the way she took that bus through the centre of town without a care for anyone else.

Uh oh. I suddenly remembered where I last saw a bus conductor. Not on our school bus. The last bus conductor I saw was in a movie. An old movie. I looked at Orsa's profile, because she was pretending not to look at me, even though one red-rimmed eye kept sliding my way. The more I thought about it, the more I was sure I was right.

'You've been put away before, haven't you?' I asked her again. 'You've been locked up for years! No wonder you got everything wrong.'

Orsa leaped to her feet, expanding a bit again as her anger rocketed, but not quite to a giant size. She tried to loom over me, screeching at the top of her lungs. 'I haven't got anything wrong! I've got everything planned. I've done my time and now you're going to get my life back for me. Just you wait and see.'

I scoffed. 'That's silly. I can't get your life back for you, whatever that even means.'

At the word silly, Orsa shrank back to normal size again, but she tried to bluff it out, feigning she had everything under control. She guffawed, but it was a pretty pathetic sound.

'Oh yes, you will! You're my hostage, stupid little flat boy. Think about it. Nobody knows where we are. No one can find us. We're going to stay hidden as long as it takes.'

'As long as what takes?' The thought of spending a lot of time with her was making me want to throw up.

'Well, that's not up to me, is it? We're going to hide until your repulsive mother comes out to save you. And then, you idiotic little man, then I will have my *vengeance*! You'll see!' she howled at me, clapping her hands together and waving them over her head.

I watched while she played out this strange little dance, but I was busy thinking, and her over-the-top displays weren't so convincing now she'd shrunk to the size of the average grandma. The magic of her enormous anger had dissolved, and she didn't seem able to call it back.

'What I see,' I said calmly, like my father explaining the reasons behind some decision I'd complained about, 'is that you're thoroughly out of date. You must have been locked away for, what, ten years? Buses don't have conductors anymore. Passengers just swipe their passes at the door. Your disguise is really, really bad. You look like an extra in an old movie, and believe me, you wouldn't get paid for this performance. What other mistakes have you made, Orsa? Do you really think nobody will find us? For pity's sake, you probably stole the bus in full view of the cameras at the depot. And I bet you didn't disable the GPS tracker on the bus, did you? And the SIM card out of my phone—did you think of that? It's in my bag on the bus. Someone will find us, and probably very soon.'

I prepared for how her reaction to my assessment of her kidnap project before I spoke, because I was pretty sure she'd get violent again. Orsa swung one meaty arm at my head, and although it didn't have quite the same heft as when she was puffed up with magical anger, it was enough to make my ears ring.

'Shut your mouth!' she roared into my face, her stinking breath like a layer of slime settling on me. She maybe looked more normal now, but she smelled like she hadn't brushed her teeth for a month. 'None of that will help you! Ten years of my life is what your bloody mother cost me, ten whole years, and today is the day she pays for it—just you wait and see.'

With that, Orsa turned her back on me and stared out the cabin door. She didn't block as much of the light now. The swelling clouds were darker, and I heard a rushing noise as if the whole structure had been dragged under the strongest spume of the waterfall. I still didn't see how kidnapping me would help this pitiful woman in any way, and I still didn't understand why she kept talking about my mother.

'My mother has gone,' I said, trying to sound composed and at least getting my voice not to shake. 'Completely gone. She's been gone ten years. Kidnapping me won't bring her back. I haven't seen her since I was a child. Whatever quarrel you had with her is long over, believe me.'

'You don't know anything,' Orsa said dismissively, waving a hand at me. 'You're an idiot boy, not worth the trouble she took over you. You're not even magic, are you? All you can do is talk to cats. Huh.'

I spoke with as much dignity as I could muster. 'I'm not as magic as some people, true. Then again, I'm not completely flat. I do have a few small magics.' Well, one small magic. But what did she know? I could claim more than I could do, surely, in front of a person as irrational as Orsa appeared to be.

She turned to shake her head at me. 'Stupid idiot boy,' she crooned with mock kindness. 'Poor little man thinks he has magic. But what does he have? Just a teeny weeny incy wincy connection with cats, fine as a thread and twice as fragile. Huh! I say, and Huh! again. Poor little chap has just enough magic to get himself into trouble, and not enough to get himself out of it. No, little boy, your piddling kitten magics can't help you. You'll have to wait for Mummy to come save you.'

'Well, that's not going to happen. She's gone, I tell you.'

'So you say.' Orsa performed her little dance, sashaying her way across the hut. She sat beside me on the wooden bench. I tried to move away, but she just jammed me into the corner. Smaller she might be, but she still reeked of foul breath and the ancient sweat of the old uniform she was wearing. Heaven knows where she got it from. 'Let's just wait and see, boy-o. I'm good at waiting. I've had ten years' practice.'

And you learned nothing, said a soft feline voice.

I jumped to my feet. 'Katkin!'

She poked her little tabby head around the hut's doorway. Behind her, the mist was clearing into a subtle spray. I could see the path and beyond it, the trees that lined the waterfall trail.

'You!' Orsa screamed, one pudgy arm pointing at our small furry visitor. 'What are you doing here? You're—you're—just you wait, you nasty little beast, just you wait!' She tugged at the magic silver bangle on her wrist, trying to pull it over her fat hand. Katkin stalked into the hut and sat with simple dignity at Orsa's feet, tucking her tail neatly around her. Looking up, she tipped her head to one side.

Silly. Bad mistake, Princess.

'I make no mistakes, you ridiculous moggy. None! Just you wait!'

The more Orsa pulled at the stuck bangle, the more deeply it stayed embedded in her puffy flesh.

Katkin sneezed. *Silly,* she repeated, almost as an aside. Then she stood and stretched ostentatiously before leaping in one bound into my arms. She butted her head under my chin and began to purr. *Tobias Felix,* she said, *Tobias Felix. Not even Princess here can take you from me.*

'How did you find me?' I asked. I glanced out the hut door, suddenly aware that there were other people there, and sirens swinging in and out of earshot.

Hush, said Katkin. *How could I find you? I'm just a cat.*

'What?' I tucked my chin in to look down at her.

She dug her claws into my jacket, stiffening her legs to mimic the pose of a frightened and skittish runaway cat who'd been lost for weeks and needed the full attention of someone kind. She meowed loudly and plaintively. I gathered her in closer and realised that someone was speaking to me— someone in uniform who was, thankfully, *not* the fake conductor. Someone who didn't need their day complicated by an encounter with a magical cat.

'Can you confirm that, please, lad? Can you hear me, son? Are you Tobias Felix Dartin?'

A stocky police officer stood directly before me, looking me carefully in the eyes. His arms were raised a little from his sides, like he was ready to grab me if I happened to fall over. Or to stop me if I tried to run. He was a little older than my dad, and he looked serious, calm, and a bit on the heavy side. Despite his age, he seemed very capable, and I had no doubt he could revive me if I fainted, or catch me if I ran. I have to say that I felt safer all of a sudden.

'Yes! Yes, that's me, all right. Thank you so much. Thank you for coming to help!'

He stepped forward and put a hand on my arm. 'Glad to be of service, son. I'm Sergeant Miller from Search and Rescue. I'll be looking after you till we get you back to your family, all right?'

I nodded, feeling a bit overwhelmed, as if someone had shone a high-beam headlight right in my face. Sergeant Miller had that kind of smile, the kind that made you relax. I even felt a small push of magic behind it, the sort that many people didn't even know they had. All the same, I was willing to bet that all his colleagues knew Miller was the one who could keep victims calm.

'All right then, young Toby,' he went on, 'let's have you out of here. The ambos need to check you over. That's a nasty bruise on your face, and your nose looks, um, broken.' The sergeant rubbed his other hand over his own rather crooked nose. 'Come out this way. No need to look at her. We have it all under control.'

I was dimly aware that there was another commotion in the hut behind me, but Sergeant Miller's aura of protection was shielding me from whatever was happening with Orsa, almost like a door had been closed behind me. He shepherded me out of the hut and onto the trail. I joined a group of uniformed personnel, surrounding me like a team of footy players around a new player. With me and Katkin in the middle, they began guiding me toward the road at the start of the track. I looked about for someone I knew, but they were all strangers. Nice strangers, but I felt odd among them. Then Katkin's claws dug into my neck, and I remembered something.

'Wait! I left something in the hut.'

'We'll fetch it for you, son, don't you worry. Come on down to the ambulance now,' Sergeant Miller said soothingly, his caring smile now just another little trick that was getting in my way. I felt bad that I couldn't respond to him, but I had no time now for his subtle magics.

Making sure I had a good hold on Katkin, I twisted to avoid the helpful hands that reached out to me. Orsa was back there in the hut, no doubt causing a huge fuss and making life very difficult for the Search and Rescue staff who found us.

What was worse, she still had the magic bangle that imprisoned Katkin for decades. There was no way I was leaving that with her.

PART FOUR
MIA

CHAPTER 16

THE TRAIL TO NOWHERE

'What now?' Dr Khan asked as Frankie moved away from the bus. 'They can't have got far!'

'No, they must be close.' Frankie looked all around, up and down the wet road leading to the lookout, and over the edge above the reservoir. We all saw Toby's little tabby cat dart into a gap in the bushes at the side of the road. Frankie pointed. 'Hang on, what about the waterfall trail?'

'Yes,' said Dr Khan. 'That's a good thought.' She took a deep breath to calm herself and then patted my shoulder. 'Coming? You're Mia, yes? Toby's friend. You go to school together, I remember.'

'That's right.' Strange that she would recognise me. We don't own any animals and I only know who she is because she visits the Dartins pretty often. 'But how do you know that? And how did you get here?'

'Toby doesn't have that many friends, you know, that he talks about. And so does Helen. Talk about you, I mean. As to how I got here, Red rang me. He'll be right along. He's just seeing if he can get a colleague to take over. Or he'll reschedule his ops—he doesn't care. Toby's more important.'

'Oh.' Well, Toby would be glad to hear that. From what Toby had told me, Mr Dartin's work was pretty vital. I knew that Toby always wanted to do well, in exams and essays and so on, to make sure he didn't give his father any worry. Toby wasn't a brainiac like Helen, but he was going to do the best he could. I never thought he needed to panic so much. Toby was really smart, but kind of nervous. Clever-nervy kids didn't always ace exams, as I knew all too well. The trick was preparation and focus. No time for nerves. While there was no way I could have prepared for the situation we faced today, focus was another thing.

'Wait a moment,' I said. 'Let's make sure we've got all the bases covered.' I heard that phrase on a television show, and I really liked it. Cover your bases. It was almost as good as being prepared. Frankie came to stand beside me, and his smile was kind without being at all superior.

'Okay, counting-est girl, let's number them off! One, we found the bus. Two, Toby isn't on it anymore. Three, little Katkin may lead us to him.'

'Yes,' I said. 'And four, there was a strange woman on the bus with him. She's probably still with him and may be dangerous. We need to be careful. So, number five, we should call the police.'

'And six, we should call an ambulance, just in case,' added Dr Khan.

'And seven, maybe one of us should stay here to let everyone know what's happening when they arrive. Dr Khan? Maybe you could do the phone calls and wait for Mr Dartin. Frankie and I will follow Katkin. I can sneak up to see what's happening, and Frankie can help out if that weird kidnapper gets violent.'

'Well, thank you,' Frankie said in mock modesty. He seemed to be ready for anything, and not the least bit afraid of whatever might lie ahead.

Dr Khan, on the other hand, looked as spooked as a grown woman could. She blinked at me. 'Maggie. Call me Maggie.' Then she took another deep breath. 'I'm just no good at this. Never have been. Crisis time. I hate it. People in danger. It terrifies me. Just thinking of Toby!'

'Don't think about him. Just call triple zero,' I said. 'Please, Dr—I mean, please, Maggie.'

She gave a shaky smile and nodded. 'Of course. I left my phone in the car, but I'll get right onto it.'

Dr Khan turned and crossed back to where her Jeep was parked behind Frankie's little orange number, kind of in the middle of the road, definitely blocking the carriageway. She'd remembered to put the hazards on, which I thought was pretty awesome for someone who claimed to be hopeless in a crisis. At least any traffic would see her and be able to avoid the stricken bus up ahead.

'Ohhhh-kaaay,' Frankie said in that slightly annoying way of his. He rubbed his hands together, ready for action. 'What now? Try to follow the cat?' He cleared his throat, and I realised that he was a lot more scared than he wanted to let on.

'Yes. I think that cat will know where to find Toby,' I said. 'I hope. Anyway, it's a plan and right now it's the only one we've got.'

I pushed my glasses more firmly onto my nose and led the way. Katkin had darted into the undergrowth at the side of the track that went up to the waterfall. It was a track I knew well, because it was a favourite picnic spot for my little brothers. We came up here a few times every year, bringing a big basket of food, a thermos full of tea, and all sorts of games and toys that the little ones could amuse themselves with. There was a big wooden hut where we usually stopped for a cuppa and a snack on the way up, and at the top there was a cleared space where the boys could wrestle and kick a ball around. Last year, the council replaced the old wooden railings with a proper wire fence, and resurfaced the path, so it was pretty easygoing, even when Mum was pregnant with Lucky Day, or afterward just carrying her in the sling.

We walked along, trying to avoid the wet fronds of tree fern that dripped the last of the rain onto us. In summer, this track is shady and very pleasant, and popular with other families. We hadn't been up here for a while. It seemed to me that everyone was busier than before, with the boys playing different sports on the weekends, and me doing extra study in the afternoons while they stayed on at after-care. Dad was always late home and Mum was exhausted from full-time work and taking care of Lucky Day. *We really should try to get out more.* A picnic would be fun, as soon as the weather improved. The waterfall trail would be smooth enough for Lucky Day's pusher this summer, with the nice newly surfaced path and all. I thought about what kind of food I would help Mum make to bring along.

I thought about everything except how bad things could be for Toby, trying to stay calm as I could. Then I looked ahead and stopped walking.

'What's that?' I asked in a kind of stage whisper to Frankie behind me.

Frankie stood at my shoulder. He had almost walked into me. 'What's what?' he whispered back. I'm not sure why we did that, except that the air seemed full of strangeness.

I screwed up my eyes and blinked. I took my glasses off and rubbed the lenses on the hem of my jumper, which I know I'm not supposed to do, and pushed them back on to my nose. The lenses were now dry, but I still couldn't make sense out of what I was seeing.

'That, that shimmery thing. Where the hut should be. Hang on, where the hut is. Oh, it's gone again. It's gone behind the— What on earth *is* that?'

Frankie clicked his tongue. 'Don't see it,' he said in an annoyed voice. 'Strange. I can't see the hut, but I don't see anything shimmering. Just a bit of mist from the waterfall.'

'Too much mist!' I told him. 'The waterfall's not even running all that heavily. And the hut keeps fading in and out.'

'Ohhhh-kaaay,' said Frankie. He stepped around me and began to walk forward again, very slowly, arms lifted from his sides, as if with each step he might set off a mine. 'I wonder,' he said for the millionth time that morning.

'Will you please stop wondering and tell me what you are thinking?' I hissed. If I kept my eyes really narrowed, I could just about make out the hut, mostly hidden in the flickering mist.

When Frankie's silhouette was between me and the hut, his shape gave it a firmer outline, separate from the eye-watering sparkle.

'Wait!' I said, grabbing the back of his coat. 'What's that noise?' Somewhere up ahead, some sort of ruckus was going on —shouting, kicking, crunching, shrieking.

Frankie spoke over his shoulder. 'It's just the waterfall.'

Then someone yelled. The words were indistinct, but whoever it was sounded very angry indeed.

'Okay. Not the waterfall then,' said Frankie. 'Somebody's trying to confuse us by using magic. We'd better be careful.'

'We'd better be quick!' I added, squirming round to the front. I took a couple of steps before Frankie grabbed my shoulder.

'Wait!'

He got me just in time to stop me from falling into a very large crack that had opened across the path. The gap was almost two metres wide, and much deeper than I was tall. We looked down, and then we looked up. There was no sign of the hut. On the far side of the gap, the whole path was hidden by a dense, glittering mist, thicker than the waterfall splash and more colourful, like a cloud made entirely of shining gauze ribbon. All the sounds had faded, too.

I looked around in confusion. 'Where can they be? Where has the hut gone?'

CHAPTER 17

THE RESCUE TEAMS ARRIVE

Frankie shook his head and muttered crossly about being sick of dealing with random ripples of bothersome magic, cleaning up after everyone else just magicked this and magicked that without a single thought for the consequences. He even shook his fist at the sparkly cloud, as if that would make a bit of difference.

'Frankie,' I said, taking hold of his arm, 'I think we have to get over there. Whoever that odd woman is, and whatever it is she wants with Toby, the answer is over there.'

He took a deep breath and nodded. 'You're right, counting girl. Mia,' he corrected. 'Now, how to get across? We need a branch or something.'

We looked about the trail. Unlike how it used to look, it was tidy and had neat edges, with the bush plants all trimmed back, apart from the rain-heavy fern fronds that leaned down and dripped overhead. Unfortunately, the orderly rangers had removed all the offcuts of both the trees and the shaped timber they'd used for the new fence. I was just thinking about whether I could make it across the crack by jumping if I had a really, really good run-up, when we heard a shout from behind us.

'Hoy, there!' called a man dressed in orange. SES was written in large black letters on the front of his bright helmet.

State Emergency Services. Good.

'Hoy!' he said again, and 'Stop! Stay there!' even though we were standing perfectly still. He sounded quite breathless, like he'd been running from a long distance away.

I heard a patchy blare of sirens echoing up the side of the mountain. The emergency crews had definitely arrived. Dr Khan—I mean, Maggie—must have been very quick on the phone, or maybe they'd already been alerted by the carnage in the streets and the very public speeding of the bus right through town. At least they were here. I was grateful for that, however it happened.

It was hard to keep still as we waited impatiently for Orange Overalls to get to us. When he arrived, I saw that he looked very young. He was all red in the face, sweaty and pimply and earnest. *Oh great, they sent the cadets, when we need someone who knows what to do.*

'Adrian Pickles,' he said, nodding to Frankie and me. 'SES. We can take over from here. Police Search and Rescue are on their way. Anything we need to know?'

For someone who looked so young—well, maybe he was about eighteen—he sounded very confident, so that made me feel a bit better. Of course I was relieved that help was here, but it was annoying that Orange Adrian wanted to push us aside. Luckily Frankie answered him while I was still working out what to say.

'We think the woman from the bus has taken our friend to the waterfall hut. The problem is, we can't see the hut properly, and now there's a great gap in the path. We're just figuring out how to get over it.'

Adrian looked around in a summing up kind of way, like a teacher checking to see if everyone was on the same page. He looked at the trees over our heads, then along the path toward the hut, then down at the little chasm below the new gap in the track, the whole time with a serious expression on his face. He pulled up his collar and spoke into the communication device clipped there. We heard his half of the strange rescue-team conversation.

'Hi Sarah, Adrian … Yep, that's right … Yep. Yep … Ropes and tackle, yep … Two public … Under control … No worries, send the others up … I'll wait here.'

He listened for a few seconds more, his gaze turned up to the trees overhead, and then clicked the comms switch off. He cleared his throat and nodded to us, blue eyes bright with purpose in his pimply red face.

'Police Rescue team's almost here,' he said in an obvious attempt to reassure us. 'Now I know you don't wanna hear this, but you two are kind of gonna be in the way. You know, you're just two more people to take care of, two people we don't need on the ground. Comms centre says you shouldn't be here. So if you could both go back down to the road and wait with the doctor lady, that would be great.'

Frankie looked at me, eyebrows raised. I shook my head.

'No way,' I said. 'We can take care of ourselves. Thank you all the same. We'll just wait right here. We won't get in anyone's way, but Toby might need us. And so might Katkin.'

Adrian blinked at me. 'Katkin? Who's that? Are there two kids lost?'

'No, no. Katkin is Toby's pet cat. Don't worry about it now,' Frankie said soothingly. 'It's Toby who's most important. Just think of us as two extra volunteers, okay? No hindrance to anyone. Maybe we can be helpful when you rescuers bring him down here.'

Adrian nodded slowly, narrowing his eyes at Frankie. 'Hmm. All right. That's the spirit. Just don't get in anyone's way, right? Here they come.'

Frankie and I pressed ourselves against the trees on the high side of the trail as a dozen uniformed Search and Rescue staff slogged up to us. Unlike Adrian, with his shocking orange overalls, the Police Search and Rescue team were all in white. Each of them had different badges and equipment hanging off them, and white helmets with gold shields on the front. They looked like firefighters, but all in white.

The older man in the lead tucked in beside us as the rest of the crew went past. They had an instant solution to the problem of the gap in the trail—a narrow length of perforated metal laid down to use as a bridge.

The guy in charge said to Frankie, 'You'd both be better off waiting with your friend down on the road, you know.' He held up a hand as Frankie protested. 'It's all right, son. I understand. Just don't get in the way, and obey any instructions young Pickles here gives you, agreed?'

He turned to Adrian, talking about us as if we couldn't hear him. 'They seem calm enough at the moment. If they get hysterical, call for another of your crew and walk them down the mountain quick smart. Otherwise, sometimes it's helpful to have a known face nearby. All clear?'

'Yes, Sarge,' Adrian replied.

The sergeant nodded, then gave us a smile, one which made me feel better. He was really reassuring. 'Just wait here, folks. We'll have your boy back in no time.' With a whistle to his troops up ahead, he crossed the flimsy makeshift bridge and disappeared into the mist.

'What now?' I asked.

'Now we wait,' Frankie and Adrian said together.

Waiting is the hardest thing ever.

We waited for ages. A couple of times, Adrian Pickles walked a few steps away from us, muttering into his comms unit. He seemed to be the link person for the police team, and every now and then he got a message from the SES squad leader over the comms unit. Mostly we stood looking at each other without saying anything, just listening to the fluctuating nee-naw of sirens behind us and the muffled shouts from up ahead.

I didn't look at my watch, but I'm sure it was many horrendously long minutes until we saw any progress. I took off my glasses twice to clear them of drips from the trees, but it still took ages to see anything helpful. Slowly, the gauzy cloud thinned, and the hut came into clear view again. And it wasn't all that far ahead; it made no sense that it had been invisible. I could see the white overalls of the rescue team gathered around it. I thought about just walking up to join them, calling out to Toby.

Then the shouting grew plainer, and I made out some of the words. They didn't make me feel any better.

The strange woman was yelling with the most awe-inspiring menace in her voice. She sounded like the last person on earth anyone would want to be near. *Just you wait*, and *you idiot boy*, she cried in a way that seemed to threaten extreme and immediate danger to poor Toby. Hearing somebody call out, *ma'am, let go of him now*, gave me the shudders. I tried not to imagine exactly what was happening. Frankie patted my shoulder to calm me down, but as he was doing a kind of anxious jig at the same time, it didn't really work.

A moment later, we saw the police sergeant stride into the hut. Two other officers followed. Now that they were inside, I couldn't catch anything they were saying. I needed to get closer, but remembered that I would have to go over that skinny piece of perforated metal that crossed the yawning gap. I looked down, readying myself to step onto the narrow bridge.

The metal plank lay on a perfectly whole path. 'How did that …?' I started to ask, then realised it didn't matter a bit. I was with Frankie; these silly magic flourishes were really annoying. I ran forward, avoiding the outstretched arm that young Pickles tried to throw in front of me. I dashed up toward the hut, Pickles and Frankie jogging behind me, calling out for me to stop. By the time I reached the team milling around the hut entrance, I saw Toby already being escorted out by the sergeant. I almost fell over; I was so relieved to see he was on his feet and fine. Fine, despite a blackening eye and a bloody nose. I felt faint from gratitude. Toby was practically unharmed.

Frankie blew a relieved whistle behind me as the police rescue team began guiding Toby toward us down the track. I took a deep, steadying breath and clasped my hands together to keep from saying anything mushy. Toby was safe, and Katkin was draped across his shoulder.

Everything was going to be all right. Any moment now, he would see us and know that we'd been looking for him. I'd catch his eye, and we'd smile our relief and pretend we weren't embarrassed by all the fuss. Soon we'd be swapping stories of what a horrible day it had been.

Toby would probably say something funny about bus-napping being the most original way he'd ever managed to skive off school for a day.

I'd tell him not to make a habit of it.

Frankie would say ohhh-kaay.

But, while I was waiting and imagining all this, playing out a whole conversation in my head and counting my in-out breaths to slow down my thumping heart, Toby suddenly ducked out from under the helping hands of the police officers. He said something that didn't make sense, mumbling about something he couldn't leave behind. Before any of the police could react, he slipped away from them and sprinted back to the hut.

I couldn't wait any longer. I'm not even sure how I did it, but I was almost the first to follow him. In seconds, I was crowded into the small hut with every officer of the rescue team, a stunned-looking sergeant, red-faced Adrian Pickles, and Frankie too.

But that's all.

Apart from the whole gang of us staring at each other and looking about as if we couldn't believe our eyes, the hut was empty. Even the two police officers who had stayed in the hut looked totally dazed. Nobody could work out what had happened. No Toby, no kidnapper, no little tabby cat.

Empty wooden hut, trampled dirt floor, a few stray raindrops making their way through the thatch of the roof. The silence of disbelief, a couple of suppressed swear words. *What the?*

I bit my lip and growled my frustration.

PART FIVE
TOBY

CHAPTER 18

KATKIN IS OVERMATCHED

Yes! Katkin said as I escaped from my rescuers and tore back to the hut. *Get it, Tobias! Don't let her keep the bangle.*

Two Search and Rescue officers were in there with Orsa. They were trying to calm her down and asking her to come quietly. As far as I could see, she wasn't paying them the least bit of attention. I put a hand on Katkin to hold her steady, because she'd bunched herself to leap from my grasp and scratch Orsa's eyes out, and I didn't want her to get anywhere near that woman. I turned and slipped sideways between the two officers to get in front of them.

'Orsa!' I shouted. 'It's all over, whatever game you're playing. The police have this place surrounded, and whatever you think, you are back in custody. Give me that bangle, now!'

'Haha!' she cackled, holding her arm high, her left hand supporting her right wrist where the silver bangle seemed to have grown very heavy. 'Not so fast, little man.'

'Step back, please, young sir,' said one police officer, while the other spoke to Orsa.

'Ma'am, give over,' she said. She had handcuffs ready to

secure the prisoner. 'Time to head back to the station. You'll have every opportunity to explain yourself.'

'Haha!' Orsa said again in her best bad-lady voice. She really seemed very fond of overacting. 'Not going to read me my rights? Naughty, naughty little police girl. Perhaps you'd better start again, sweetie.'

The police officer looked offended at being called 'sweetie'. She frowned heavily and stepped toward Orsa, who had her back pressed against the far wall of the hut. 'Really, ma'am—'

She stopped speaking mid-sentence, and I looked at her in surprise. She was now perfectly still, one hand outstretched, handcuffs ready in the other. Her eyes had gone glassy and her breathing sounded laboured. Her fellow officer was in exactly the same state, gasping for air like a stranded fish, motionless as a statue. As I watched, his lips started to turn blue.

'What have you done? What have you done to them?' I demanded. 'Stop it, Orsa, stop it right now!'

Katkin screeched and flung herself out of my arms. She clambered up Orsa's uniform, wailing like an air-raid siren, striking out with her claws at every opportunity. Orsa laughed, still holding her wrist out of the little cat's reach.

'Be careful, furry beast,' she crooned. 'Want the bangle, do you? Keep scratching me and you can have it as your home for all time.'

Katkin dropped to the floor, looking stunned. Although she didn't start to struggle for breath like the police officers, her eyes went wide with fright, the pupils huge and black. *No, no,* she cried. *No!* It sounded like she was screaming inside my head. The idea of Katkin trapped forever in that circlet of silver was horrifying, and made me gasp too.

My thoughts were exploding so quickly, it was hard to catch one long enough to make sense of it. Cracked ideas rushed through my mind. I stepped between Katkin and Orsa, and made myself grab the lapels of Orsa's stupid, musty, outdated conductor uniform.

'What is it you want?' I asked. 'You still haven't said. Why are you doing all this? Killing police, running over pedestrians, torturing cats, kidnapping me? For heaven's sake, say what it is you want!'

'So *now* you ask!' Orsa boomed. 'What do I care for a few flats? For a hundred flats? They may as well be ants. If they get in my way, they will suffer. It's that simple.'

I chanced a look sideways at each of the police officers. Only seconds had passed, because they were both still on their feet, but I knew it couldn't be long before they passed out and died from lack of oxygen.

I pulled Orsa very close. 'Let them live. For me. You want me for something, that much is clear. If you stop choking them, I'll come with you.'

Orsa narrowed her eyes. 'You'll come with me in any case.' She flicked one hand at the police behind me. 'Those flats could never stop me, idiot boy!'

'No, they'll be dead,' I said between gritted teeth. 'And you'll be a murderer. And I will raise all hell while you try to get me out of here.'

'You!' she scoffed. 'You, raise hell? You wouldn't know how, little man.'

'I'm learning quickly,' I panted. Orsa responded with her melodramatic Joker laugh again.

In truth, I had no idea what I could possibly do to make her escape more difficult. She'd already shown that she was more than a match for me in physical strength, at least when she was blown up with magical fury. I felt Katkin clamber up the back of my jeans and leap onto my shoulder.

We just won't move, she prompted, and nosed my left ear to emphasise her point.

I nodded, much to Orsa's surprise. 'I'm not moving until you let these two breathe again.'

With Katkin's strong encouragement, I planted my feet and stiffened my legs. I forced my shaking body to stillness. I counted my breaths, slowly, the way Mia showed me to calm my exam nerves. I thought about how it might feel to be a tree, to be immoveable, to be anchored to the floor of the hut. I thought about how the dirt under my feet was packed hard over the rocks below, how the clever roots of the nearby mountain ash trees bound it all together, how years of use and weather had made everything a seamless whole. A whole that I was now a part of. A complete connection that soothed and sustained me.

Orsa screamed in frustration. 'Stop it!' she cried. She put her hands up over her ears, as if someone else was making the horrible moans escaping from her own mouth. 'Stop it! Stop the magic!'

'Um, you first,' I said.

As far as I knew, the only magic I was performing was to stand very, very still, thinking about how I was part of the landscape. I deliberately steered away from the thought that whatever I was doing might have a touch of magic about it. It was just me, with Katkin's help, becoming part of the scenery. Just me, me and Katkin, keeping very, very, very still.

Orsa shrieked again, raising both arms in the air. One after the other, the police officers fell to the ground. Immediately, I let my grip on the dirt floor release. I dropped to my knees by the one who was nearest to me, Katkin sticking close by my side. The officer was breathing again, but although his eyes were open, he didn't seem to see us. The other officer was in a similar state. Just as we reached her side, she stirred and started to gather herself.

'What the ... what ...' she began, but at that moment, there was a yank on my shoulder that threw me off balance.

'Come on then, idiot boy,' Orsa said roughly. 'We're out of here. No heroics, mind. You gave me your word.'

Katkin scrambled inside my jacket, perhaps hoping that Orsa had forgotten her. The little cat didn't make a sound in the cold dimness of the hut, or even breathe a word in my mind. I stumbled to my feet and followed my horrible kidnapper through a flapping board behind the bench. She had a tight hold on my sleeve, a bruising grip on my upper arm.

'Where to now?' I asked.

'Keep quiet,' she hissed, underlining her command with a heavy slap to the back of my head. 'This way! I've done my homework, school boy. I know all the trails up here. No one will *ever* find us.'

She dragged me toward the steep slope that led away from the back of the hut, down to the reservoir picnic area. I lurched after her, being as clumsy as possible, deliberately breaking branches and knocking against tree ferns, hoping to leave a trail. Orsa noticed what I was trying to do and gave me a solid kick to remind me that she was in charge. I rubbed at my aching thigh and blundered along behind her, down the switchbacks of the track, staggering against the logs and rocks that narrowed the path every now and then. We were soon out of earshot of the waterfall, and Orsa paused to catch her breath. I bent over, leaning my hands on my knees, gasping a little with pain and frustration. I'd been so close to being rescued that I couldn't bear to think about it.

'I still don't get it,' I said. 'What's the point if nobody will ever find us?'

'Only one person needs to,' Orsa answered with an ugly leer. 'Your smarty pants, pretty-face mother. She'll sniff us out, the bitch, and then! Then! Then I will have every drop of my revenge.' Again, the evil, over-done laugh.

'You really are strange,' I told her. 'I'll go wherever you ask, but you won't get my mum to come. She's long gone, I tell you, completely disappeared. She might even be dead for all I know.'

Orsa stared at me, her eyes suddenly open wide. 'No,' she whispered. 'No, that can't be!' Releasing her hold on me, she drifted a few steps away.

While I shook myself into better order and made sure Katkin was fine in her hiding place, Orsa paced up and down as well as she could on the narrow path. The possibility that my mother might be dead had evidently never occurred to her. On odd occasions, I actually felt better when I imagined that my mother died sometime when I was little. I knew that sounded strange—who would want to imagine their mother dead?—but at times it was a more comfortable idea than knowing she had walked away from us all.

Maybe Orsa was able to tell me more about my mother's reasons for disappearing. She evidently had some history with my mother that I knew nothing about. I felt a strange, uncomfortable tightness in my chest, like I might start to cry. I clenched my teeth until the feeling passed.

Finally Orsa grunted and came back to where I was standing.

'She can't be,' she informed me. 'I'd know. Someone would know. Someone would have told me. Mind you ... perhaps ... Huh.'

I had a sinking feeling, worse than before. I threw those words out without thinking about their meaning, other than they might upset Orsa's plans, whatever they were. Now the notion that my mother might actually be dead—and I not know it—froze my heart.

'Perhaps what?' I asked hollowly.

'Perhaps nothing. Come along. In fact, go in front of me. Just follow the path. I need to think.'

I did as I was told, wondering what the result of Orsa's thoughts might be. Thinking didn't seem to be her strong suit, all in all. Tucked between my shirt and jumper, covered by my jacket, Katkin risked the thinnest of whispers. *Not dead,* she reassured me.

I stumbled and almost fell, catching myself in time to avoid Orsa's arm as she thumped me in the back every now and again to keep me moving. I held Katkin's words to myself, not quite sure that it was my mother she was talking about, but somehow feeling better.

Behind me, Orsa grunted in a very irritating manner as she contemplated who knew how many loopy notions. When I looked over my shoulder, she waved her arms at me, and I turned back to the front and kept climbing.

CHAPTER 19
THE CROW CAVE

We walked for ages, with me leading the way and Orsa prodding me onto the right path. Eventually, both of us needed to take a private break—as private as that might be with Orsa turning her eyes away while she held a fistful of my jacket. Any hopes I had of escape seemed useless, because Orsa was so sly herself that she was always at least two steps ahead of me in the sneaky stakes.

Besides, I'd agreed to go with her. I wasn't sure if her being wicked and evil was enough reason not to honour my promise, but I certainly thought hard about it.

Some of the side paths we took were so narrow that they were clearly not part of the park's network. They looked like wallaby or wombat trails, all overgrown with long tangles of razor grass and blackberry, uneven and difficult to cover. I was glad Katkin was hidden away safely, even as I cursed the paper-thin cuts the grass inflicted on my hands and face, and stumbled over blackberry canes set like barbed traps across our route.

I'd been to the reservoir picnic grounds before, but never this way. It felt like we were going around the back of the mountain somehow, but the bush was so dense it was impossible to tell where we were.

All I knew was that I couldn't hear any sirens or traffic on the road behind us. Although the rain stopped hours ago, it was getting dark, and the wind started to pick up again. Rescue seemed impossible now. I missed my chance, and Orsa was going to win. I didn't know what it was she wanted to win, but I couldn't see any way of preventing her from achieving it.

My mother couldn't even know that this was happening, let alone get here from wherever she was. I'd never known where she went, but Dad said she wouldn't ever come to visit, that she could never come to our house again. She must be really far away, or else decided that she didn't want anything to do with us anymore.

And I cursed myself for going back to the hut. That was stupid. We were safe, Katkin and I, safe for just a few minutes in the care of that nice police rescue sergeant with the bit of magic in his smile.

Not safe, came a tiny thread of comment. *Bangle.*

Oh.

Yes, of course. As long as Orsa had the magic bangle, none of us would be quite safe. I remembered what Uncle Rain said about something going wrong in the magic world or the flat world. I guessed this was it. Only he was wrong. It wasn't the flat world *or* the magic world. Orsa was making things go wrong in both worlds. I slogged on, just telling myself to keep going. When we got to wherever it was that we were going, maybe I'd have a chance to do something.

It didn't help that part of my brain couldn't think of anything else but the lunch packed carefully into my backpack. I could hear my stomach grumbling above the slogging of my footsteps.

When the last of the light was sliding down between the

trees, going on became even more dangerous. Stupidly so. I stopped directly in Orsa's way.

'It's getting dark. Are you planning to spend the night sitting in the open on this kangaroo track?'

Orsa put both hands on her hips. 'Look behind you, idiot boy. 'You'll find we have a nice little cave all to ourselves. Here we are in Babylon!'

I turned to stare at the surrounding bush. In the dimming light, I could just make out a rocky outcrop between the trees, a place known locally as Babylon Rock. It was a bit like Hanging Rock, but hidden here among the trees instead of standing proudly on a hilltop. Huge granite boulders heaved out of the ground, leaning together like they were plotting something, as if they knew secrets they would never share. Their crowns were so closely linked that scrubby vegetation had colonised their tops, hanging down like grey-green curls on stony bald heads, high above us. Native clematis draped down in tendrils, starred with small white flowers, and snarls of blackberry made a dangling curtain of thorns. At the base of the enormous boulders, black shadows showed where there might be a hollow between or under them, and there was the tell-tale tinkle of a tiny stream running between two of the sentinel rocks. As far as I could tell, Orsa and I would need to go down on all fours to find our way inside whatever cavern the great grey slabs concealed.

'In there? That's our spot for the night? Are you serious? Do you have food and drink in there for us?'

Before Orsa could answer, a strident chorus of crows arrived directly overhead, their cawing so loud it was like being hit with a jackhammer.

I put my hands over my ears. *Ow!*

Katkin scrambled (using her ever-so-sharp claws) up my chest and pushed her neat tabby head out into the fresh air. She started meowing repeatedly at the top of her power, but the sound was almost completely drowned by the enthusiastic efforts of the crows, a massive number of them. A murder of crows, I remembered from my primary school list of collective nouns. Murder wasn't a sufficiently noisy word. This lot would be better called a cannonade of crows. Another random thought reminded me how Mia once told me that these birds were not actually the same as European crows, but should be called 'little crows', a separate Australian member of the crow family. Fine, they could have a separate collective noun.

A din of little crows. A boom of little crows. No, an ear-split of little crows.

With the ruckus showing no signs of diminishing, I looked across at Orsa. If I was finding the racket painful to hear, she was in an even worse state. With her arms flailing above her head, she was shouting at the birds to go away, using language that was too colourful even for Helen to consider.

Weirdly, the more she yelled, the nearer those crows came. Some landed in the branches around us, so close that I could have reached out and run my hand over their glossy black wings spread wide as they screamed the alarm. A couple of larger ones were taking turns diving almost into Orsa's face, worse than any swooping magpie. Orsa's curses turned into screams, and she curled into herself to avoid the crows' beaks and claws.

I could hardly believe what I was seeing. Orsa started to shrink smaller and smaller. Her whole body folded away from the striking birds, like an echidna rolling into a ball.

She looked pitiful and helpless, a tiny defenceless creature attacked by a vicious horde. She was squealing, and it sounded exactly like a terrified cat, like Tenner's kittens when she couldn't get to them.

Pity flared inside me, not for the Orsa who kidnapped and

punched and kicked and abused me, but for this poor little creature being mobbed by predatory birds. I opened my mouth to cry out, to yell at the birds to leave her alone, or something equally dumb, when a hush descended on the scene. An aching quiet and a dense, swelling darkness. Night had fallen, and in that instant, the crows backed off. The tremendous flapping of their wings as they lifted away from us sounded like fruit bats startled out of the pines in the botanic gardens.

Or a helicopter taking off nearby.

Day birds, Katkin explained. *Not night.*

Of course.

The dark was growing more solid, but my eyes were adjusting to the gloom just as quickly. Even though it was always darker in the bush than in town, if you closed your eyes for a few seconds and opened them again, you'd see that the night wasn't quite as black as it seemed when you first stepped into it. Orsa was stirring, gathering herself together to stand, and her body was resuming a normal adult size.

My impulse to protect her from the crows completely disappeared, turned off in the instant the crows flapped away. I ground my teeth, angry with myself for ever having wished to save her.

Then I noticed a stray gleam in the growing darkness. The silver bangle was on the path beside her; it must have come loose and slipped off her wrist when she shrank.

I darted down and grabbed it.

As I stood up again, I slid it over my hand. The bangle was warm and felt almost alive. It seemed to hum and purr as it adjusted to the exact size of my wrist.

Yes! said Katkin, bouncing on all four paws like a cartoon dog waiting for a treat. *Thank you, thank you Tobias!*

'No-o-o-o-o-o!' Orsa shrieked, her voice echoing off the rocky custodians of Babylon.

PART SIX
MIA

CHAPTER 20

KIDNAP PHASE TWO

Several hours later, we still didn't know exactly what had happened.

Sergeant Miller, the policeman in charge of the Search and Rescue team, pointed out a damaged panel at the back of the hut, which was how, everyone guessed, Orsa had taken Toby away.

Unfortunately, it took everyone far too long to realise that Toby and the strange conductor woman had disappeared, and which way they had gone. No one could find any sign of them around the hut, and the only thing they could do was to send out the entire Search and Rescue group to scout around the bushland near the waterfall.

There was only one main track up to the lookout, but plenty of smaller trails led to particular rock features, down to the reservoir, or just into the bush where there were lots of picnic spots.

There were so many trails Toby and the kidnapper could have taken. It seemed an impossible task. I didn't have a good feeling about it.

Sometime not long after lunch, they brought in search dogs

and a helicopter, though the wet and windy weather didn't really suit either of them. The rain was washing away any scent trail that the dogs might have followed, and visibility was low for the helicopter team, Sergeant Miller explained.

Frankie and I spent the hours waiting with Maggie and Mr Dartin back at command headquarters—a small caravan set up by the side of the road. The bus had been towed away, and both Frankie's car and Maggie's Jeep were now parked neatly beside the trail, next to Mr Dartin's sedan. The road to the lookout was closed to traffic, except for residents and emergency personnel being allowed through. There were a couple of reporters waiting for news back at the roadside barrier, apparently.

I phoned my mum, and the police promised her they would bring me home as soon as they could. That would be either when Toby was found or when I'd told them as much as I knew about what had happened. They kept asking for extra details about Toby, about me, about school, about our ordinary days, about what happened this morning, about what happened on usual mornings. It didn't seem like they would ever be finished with questions.

A paramedic put a blanket around my shoulders as if I was hurt. I wasn't hurt, but I was shaking all the same. The shaking went on for quite a while. Somebody brought sandwiches and biscuits and coffee too, and I think I ate something without even realising it.

Toby's dad sat beside me with his head in his hands, and on my other side, Maggie had one arm over my shoulders. Frankie sat the far side of Toby's dad, making quiet comments and trying to be positive. We told our stories about half a dozen times, but there were always more questions. When it began to grow dark, Sergeant Miller returned to speak to us again.

He looked at Toby's dad. 'Mr Dartin, I'm sorry to ask this, but it would help if we went through it all one more time. A detective has arrived from Melbourne who'd like to speak with you. With you all.' He looked at each of us in turn and smiled, just a bit. There was something so kind about his smile that I relaxed. He made it seem that going through everything for the thirtieth time would be useful somehow, as if the new guy from the city would solve the mess immediately. Sergeant Miller went on a bit more.

'Inspector Gray was on the original Mussari case, so you might know him, Mr Dartin. Sir, Toby's father is in here.' He moved out of the way to let the new guy in.

The detective was a grey-haired man in a grey suit and grey tie, with a grey beard. He pulled up a folding chair and sat opposite us. Everything about him was grey. He really lived up to his name.

'Mr Dartin? I'm Bob Gray. You might remember me?'

Toby's dad nodded. His lips were pulled tight, and he looked like he might cry. I hated that look on his face. It made me feel scared again.

But he answered the policeman briskly. 'Yes. I remember. How are you, Detective? Or should I say, Inspector?'

'Bob will do,' the inspector said with a quirk of his thin lips, which might have been a sort of smile once upon a time. He looked like a man who didn't smile much. 'Now, let's recap the situation. This is what I understand—please feel free to add anything or correct anything I get wrong, all right? Good. Let's start at the beginning.'

He leaned forward so that his elbows rested on his knees, making sure to look each of us in the eye. 'From what Miss Lam here tells us,' he said, 'the kidnapper is a middle-aged woman with wild hair, an angry demeanour, and a red face. She looked extremely tall, but then she was high up in the bus. So despite the discrepancy in size, and her previous obsession with a fashionable appearance, we think it is most probably Orsa Mussari, playing out her grudge against your family, sir.'

I had learned a bit about this woman over the course of the afternoon, but there was still a lot I didn't know. I listened carefully.

'You can still call me Red, you know,' Toby's dad said to the inspector. 'My brother and I are sure that it *is* Orsa Mussari come back to torment us.' He sounded tired and exhausted, like he was in pain. 'We all hoped we'd heard the last of her. Now it looks like she's back, trying to ruin our lives again. What we don't understand is, I mean, I don't want to sound too critical, but can you tell us how this happened? How this was *allowed* to happen?'

Inspector Gray pursed his lips. 'Don't ask me to start describing the legal system, Red,' he said dryly. 'And how my hands might be tied. But you do deserve an explanation, such as it is. This is what we know.'

He started to tick off his fingers as he gave out bits of information, which I found reassuring, because he looked to know everything he needed to know. 'Mussari recently completed her minimum ten years, right? She then convinced the governors that she was safe to be let out. Everyone was confident—that includes me, I have to confess, for my part. They did ask my opinion about whether she was a danger to your wife. As far as we know, from all we can see in official records, there was no way she could trace your wife. Jenny has disappeared even deeper than witness protection could dig. Nobody at all knows where she is.' He looked expectantly at Mr Dartin.

Toby's dad gave the saddest smile I have ever seen. 'That's right,' he agreed. 'Jenny is untraceable. I haven't seen or heard from her in over ten years, and I don't envisage seeing or speaking to her again. Ever. None of us expects to.'

I put a hand to my mouth. I had never heard anyone sound

so desolate. Maggie patted my shoulder, and I blinked back the sudden spring of tears to my eyes.

Inspector Gray nodded. His face was grave. 'As I thought. And from the discussions we had back then, we didn't anticipate that Mussari would target your family; am I right? That she would only ever go after your wife. I'm sure that's what we all decided. That was the reason Jenny disappeared so completely, at least as we understood your situation. She did it deliberately, so that you would all be safe.'

Toby's dad sighed heavily. 'That was her plan.'

A silence fell. I was having trouble following this conversation completely, and I saw that Frankie looked a bit confused, too. Maggie reached over me to put her hand on Mr Dartin's shoulder.

'Red,' she prompted. 'Maybe Frankie and Mia need a bit of background here.'

Toby's dad buried his face in his hands. 'You do it,' he muttered. 'I can't—I just can't talk about it. Please.'

'Is it all right with you, Inspector? These two have been chasing Toby all day.'

'Go ahead. There's nothing to hide now. Anything they can add, any small thing they've noticed, might just help us in the search. Secrets are chancy things at the best of times, and we can't afford them now.'

'Thank you.' Maggie turned sideways so she could take both my hands in hers. Frankie pulled his chair closer.

'Now, Mia, I'm not sure how much Toby has told you about his mum. Or you either, Frankie.'

Frankie shrugged. 'I think I have parts of the story. It's, er, quite well known in certain circles. But I never asked for a full explanation. I just wanted to help, and I've been glad to do that the last few years.'

'I know,' said Maggie. 'You've been a godsend. Anyway, in a

nutshell, Orsa Mussari went to university with us—with me, Red, Rain, and Jenny. She wasn't quite in our group, but just on the edge. She was very beautiful and very rich, with the most beautiful clothes to flaunt, doing amazing internships at all the best accountancy firms ... Well, with all that in her favour, she should have been very popular, but she had, er, some very strange ideas, and some very bad connections. The long and the short of it is that she wanted to, er, get together with Toby's dad at uni. That wasn't ever going to happen, because Red and Jenny were devoted.'

At that word, Toby's dad muffled a sob and turned away from us. He got up to stand at the door of the van, looking out at the pitch black darkness while we listened to Maggie's explanation. His shoulders were hunched, and he looked so sad that I found tears coming to my eyes again.

It certainly wasn't a happy story. Maggie told it as quickly as she could. I found myself gripping her hands hard as she went on.

'Well, now. We all left uni and got on with our lives. Orsa kept trying to contact Red, and she also tried to sabotage Jenny's career. Jenny was a fine barrister, but she found it more and more difficult to ignore Orsa's attempts to ruin her. You wouldn't credit the things she got up to. Orsa would bribe witnesses, get judges changed, steal evidence, and manipulate jury selection. She seemed to have a lot of very dodgy friends in useful places, too, people who would do anything for money, and other people she could threaten and blackmail. Did I mention she was rich? Her family were builders, developers, importers, dealers, designers, all sorts of things. They had lots of huge contracts and stacks of staff and suppliers and so on, across a whole range of sectors. There was also a pile of inherited money that seemed to grow no matter how much they spent. Orsa could get hold of anyone and pay them to do anything. It got so bad that perfectly respectable clients started to take their business away from Jenny's law firm because everything they tried to do was obstructed, from building permits to divorce proceedings to inheritance disputes.'

At this point, Toby's dad turned back to us. 'Thank you, Maggie,' he said. 'I'll tell the rest. I'm pretty sure Inspector Gray might like to add something, too.'

He came back to his seat and started to tell us everything about their troubles with Orsa Mussari.

CHAPTER 21

ORSA RUINS EVERYTHING

There we sat, our heads leaning together, inside a police caravan parked on the side of a mountain. The little windows were steamed over with our breathing. At some point, a constable handed us each a mug of over-sweetened tea, and later, my dad arrived with Helen. Someone had decided it was better to bring him to me than to take me out of the scene, and for that I was very grateful.

I was glad, too, that he heard the story from somebody else, because it would have been too difficult for me to explain it myself. I was especially glad to have him beside me while Mr Dartin, Maggie, Helen, and Inspector Gray talked through the Orsa Mussari story.

It was certainly strange. And horrible.

The major problem happened during a trial when Jenny defended a man called Wilson. Wilson was accused of embezzlement. He was an accountant who worked at one of the businesses owned by Orsa Mussari. It turned out there was a lot of money passing through the business that was never properly accounted for. Enormous amounts were coming into the accounts and being siphoned off as profits, except when they looked closer at the books, the money was payment for work that never really happened. The way Toby's dad explained it, the business got millions of dollars from somewhere, deposited into the account. Then, after the money came in, they would create phoney projects with invoices to explain the deposits in retrospect. Anyway, Wilson got suspicious and alerted the authorities, and investigations began into the Mussari companies. All of them, from furriers to concreters.

'That was the last thing Orsa Mussari wanted,' Mr Dartin said. 'An absolute fortune was at stake, with the whole Mussari empire wobbling while this one investigation went on. Word got around that the authorities were looking into them, so no new orders came in because people were getting worried, and the companies couldn't afford to do any more funny business right under the noses of the forensic accountants. But before any charges could be laid against the firm's directors, the financial investigators discovered that it was Wilson himself who'd been stealing the money.'

I was stunned. 'But I thought he was the one who found the problem in the first place!' I objected. 'You mean he was the criminal all along?'

'Not at all,' said Toby's dad. 'Orsa, or her minions, had cleverly managed to doctor enough of the accounts to create a whole wad of damning evidence against Wilson. She had him charged and made sure the prosecution had piles of proof that would see him ruined and sent to prison for a very long time.'

'And Jenny heard about it,' added Maggie. 'Straightaway, she decided to defend Wilson *pro bono,* just because it was the right thing to do. And she was doing brilliantly at the trial, uncovering step-by-step the exact trail of false information that Orsa Mussari had created. Jenny understood exactly how Orsa's mind worked. We all knew how sneaky and vindictive she could be.'

'Mum did heaps of *pro bono*,' added Helen.

'Oh.' I knew about *pro bono*, where a lawyer takes on a case without being paid for it. 'So Mrs Dartin and Mr Wilson were winning. And Orsa did something?' I asked.

Toby's dad looked away. Helen squeezed his arm.

Inspector Gray started to fill in the gaps. 'Orsa Mussari was so angry by the end of the second day of the trial,' he said, 'that she decided to take matters into her own hands, to do anything she had to in order to create the result that she wanted. She waited outside the court in her car and tried to run down both Wilson and his lawyer.'

I was shocked. 'That's awful!'

There was a moment of silence.

'Wilson died,' Maggie said quietly. 'Jenny survived with only a broken leg. Wilson had seen Orsa coming and pushed Jenny out of the way as well as he could.'

'He was a good man,' said Toby's dad.

'Mussari went on the run,' the inspector said. 'But she stayed close, somehow, and she never stopped trying to kill Mrs Dartin. She never stopped trying to hurt her. She hired stalkers and hit-men. She sent dangerous packages to the house and tried to set fire to Mrs Dartin's office building in the city.'

'She tried to run down Toby, outside his school,' Helen said with a shudder. 'Another little girl was slightly injured, but a brave mum used her 4WD to block Orsa's car in the narrow street. The police were called, and Orsa Mussari was captured. I remember it clearly.'

My father shook his head in amazement. 'Such is evil,' he mumbled.

I scooted closer to him, my fold-up chair scraping across the lino. Outside, the wind had picked up and leaves and gumnuts were raining onto the tin roof of the police caravan.

'At her trial, Orsa was so shouty and violent that she had to be restrained,' Maggie said, breaking the silence again. 'Eventually, she had to be kept in prison, taking part in the trial through a video link. She swore blind that she would get Jenny, that she'd make her suffer, that she'd kill all her loved ones in front of her, just to cause her pain and anguish.'

'Threatening a witness? And she served only ten years?' asked my dad. 'For murder? Is that right?'

'Well, she was insane, you see,' Inspector Gray said, again with that dry tone to his voice. 'At least, that was what the jury decided. Not quite in her right mind when she committed manslaughter and attempted murder. She got a ten-year minimum at a psychiatric facility for the criminally insane.'

'Should have thrown away the key,' my dad muttered. 'Crazy murderer, never should've got out.' My father's words came out harshly, but I think we all agreed with his sentiments.

Inspector Gray even said, 'Quite so, Mr Lam.'

'Mum was the key prosecution witness,' Helen explained. 'With that kind of threat against her, she was supposed to go into witness protection. Usually, the whole family needs to go as well, but Mum knew it wouldn't be safe. Orsa Mussari had too many connections, in all sorts of circles. She always had a reach like you wouldn't believe. Mum couldn't see that witness protection would be safe for any of us.'

'Ohhh-kaaay,' said Frankie. He hadn't spoken for a while. 'I think I get it now. Mussari had contacts even in legal and police circles, hey? Jenny couldn't go into the official witness protection program, because the Mussari people or their contacts, or contacts of contacts or whatever, had infiltrated it. So Jenny removed herself, yes, to make sure that Orsa could never find her, never hurt her? And neither could any of Orsa's hirelings, no matter how hard they looked.'

'That's it,' said Toby's dad. 'Jenny believed that if she completely disappeared, it would be impossible for Orsa to follow. She also thought there would be no point in Orsa or her people coming after us, because Jenny would never know, so she wouldn't suffer. Immediately the trial was over, Jenny left, leaving messages for the Mussari people in places she knew they'd look. She managed to disappear completely.'

'I still don't know quite how she did that so successfully,' the inspector mused. 'I can only suppose Jenny had some pretty influential contacts herself. Whatever the case, she's done it. None of our people can find her, and I assume Orsa Mussari's searches have been just as ineffective. Jenny Dartin has vanished, as if by magic.'

I gave a little jump, which I covered by shivering like I'd suddenly got cold. I'd been thinking exactly the same thing, wondering if Jenny Dartin had used some sort of magic to disappear so completely off every radar. Or perhaps she had magical contacts, magic people who had not been corrupted by the Mussari money, people Mussari had no hold over. I was, by this time, a confirmed believer in the power of magic. I was sure that revenge-fuelled Orsa was using magic to hide Toby, and that she'd probably been using it to look for Toby's mum. She maybe used magic as well as money to make all that trouble in the first place. Anyway, no one else mentioned magic or tried to explain how Mrs Dartin had achieved her disappearance so completely.

After a few moments of silence, Toby's dad spoke again. 'Unfortunately, Orsa seems to have a new plan. Kidnapping Toby. I guess she's trying to get Jenny to come out of hiding,' he said. 'The only problem is that it can't possibly work. We have no contact with Jenny and no way to get a message to her. We can't even let her know that Toby's in danger. No matter how long Orsa hangs on to Toby, Jenny will never appear. It's so, so hopeless!' He put his head in his hands again.

'Not hopeless, sir, but taking longer than we thought. We'll find him.' The flimsy caravan door was pulled open to the windy night. Sergeant Miller stood there, looking as reliable as ever, but exhausted. Adrian Pickles was beside him, with black circles under his eyes and his red face gone very white. He was leaning heavily on the sergeant's shoulder.

Inspector Gray stood. 'No news then?'

The sergeant shook his head. 'The helicopter team's long gone, and the dogs lost the trail. Wind isn't good for them, you know, or this drizzle. Besides, it's too dangerous for any of us to continue now. This young chap's turned an ankle, so I'll take him up to the ambos. With your permission, Inspector, I'd like to call off the search until first light tomorrow.'

The inspector nodded. 'Certainly. I was just hanging on, hoping. Thank you, Sergeant. Yes, stand the troops down. We'll do better in the light.'

'Sir.' The caravan door slammed behind them, but the warmth had already escaped. There was a miserable chill in the air. I had to bite my lip again to not protest as the inspector told us all to go home, that they would be in touch, that they would keep an eye on everything. He assigned a policeman to go back to the Dartin house, to be their contact overnight.

'And we'll go home too,' said my dad. 'You'll let us know what happens, Red?'

Toby's dad shook my father's hand. 'Thanks, Vin. I'll keep you posted. Look after young Mia there; she's been a blessing today. Without her quick thinking, we wouldn't know where to start. She and Frankie did a brave thing, following that bus.'

Frankie flapped a hand, disclaiming any bravery, and my dad said, 'Ah, my Mia, she's always been the quick thinker. Good night to everyone.'

I wanted to stay on the mountain. I just wanted to be there, close to where I last saw Toby. Another part of me wanted to be safe at home with Mum and Dad and the boys all around me, and yet another wanted to go to the Dartins' place and be close to the police communications set up. I could sit next to Helen on their couch and wait the night out with her. I might find out more about the magic angle of the situation that Frankie had been talking about, that nobody mentioned in front of the police.

Or in front of my father, for that matter.

Instead, I followed my dad up the trail to the road. We drove home in silence.

CHAPTER 22

WAITING NEXT DOOR

FRIDAY

I had an uncomfortable night. Although I did sleep a bit, I kept tossing and turning and muttering, which is not such a good thing when you share a room with your three little brothers. My dad had plans to close in the back verandah to make a bedroom for me and our baby Lucky Day to share, as soon as she was old enough to have a proper bed. That night, Lucky Day was still sleeping in the cot in my parents' room, and I was, as usual, looking after the boys.

At eight years old, Jason was quiet and easy to share with, because all he ever did was read books and play with his Xbox. As for six-year-old August and five-year-old Joseph, they were every bit as bad as small boys can be: smelly, noisy, grubby, untidy, hilarious, rude, full of energy, and always making trouble. Jason and I had single beds, but the little ones shared a bunk bed. That was good for making us all fit into the room, but it meant they were forever clambering up or down to each other, throwing things between the bunks—not very accurately —booby-trapping the ladder to the top bunk, putting disgusting things into the lower bunk, hiding messy food under their bedclothes and forgetting it, stage-whispering secrets after lights-out, and generally doing their best to wreck anything that came in their reach.

I usually found August and Joseph very annoying, especially the way they left bits of Lego on the floor that were really hurtful to bare feet, or old bananas, which were even more revolting to step on.

One thing they were always good for, though, was cuddles. They loved them. At the unusual sound of me talking in my sleep, both of them landed on top of my quilt, asking if I was all right and then claiming to be cold and in need of a cuddle. So eventually I slept guarded by a small sweaty boy on either side of me, and I must admit it felt good.

In the morning, Dad popped his head into our room early, reminding us all that it was a school day and, because Aunty Belle was picking them up today, the boys had to be ten minutes ahead of their usual Aunty Joy time. Dad smiled when he realised I had a bed full of August and Joseph, and said, 'And you, Mia, take care, my girl.'

'Yes, Dad.'

Mum was already in the kitchen with Lucky Day on her hip, making all our lunches. Jason started the boys on breakfast while I got their school clothes ready. The news was on the kitchen television, and although there was a video showing the intersection where the bus had caused those collisions, there was no footage of the mountain highway or the reservoir picnic grounds. The rushed tape across the bottom of the screen declared 'Several injured by out-of-control bus', and 'Police have situation in hand', and 'Police confirm no terrorist connec-tion', and 'Mountain highway reopened', and, worst of all—as if we had bunked off school or snuck away together—'Local teens reported missing now accounted for'.

Except that Toby wasn't accounted for! Yes, at one moment, the rescue team had Toby in their hands. I knew that because I'd seen him, but I also knew they'd lost him again. I was glad to see no one had been killed by the bus, despite all the blood and mess in the Emergency Department. It made me feel a tiny bit better, but also guilty because I never thought to ask about what happened with the bus.

I made sure the boys had everything they needed while Mum finished dressing and went off to the car, Lucky Day squealing in protest because she wanted to stay and continue the annoying and extremely loud peek-a-boo game August had started with her. Aunty Belle arrived at the same time, pulling into the driveway behind Mum's station wagon, and she and Mum conducted a short but lively conversation, which I could have bet was all about me, Toby, the bus, and the police. I was sure they had a lot more to say to each other about the whole situation, when Mr Dartin's car appeared and parked across our driveway. Toby's dad stepped out, dressed in his suit, looking ready for work, and hurried up to us. I think all four of us—me, Mum, Aunty Belle, and Lucky Day—watched with our mouths hanging open as he ran the few steps toward us.

'Anna! Glad I caught you!'

'Good morning. What is it, Red?' asked my mum.

'Sorry to be a bother, but I was wondering if your Mia could help us out for a couple of hours? I know she missed a whole day of school yesterday, but Helen could help her catch up on anything, I'm sure. Oh, and Mia's books are at our place, too. I can get them if you wish ... if you'd rather,' he said. I remembered I had emptied my backpack in the Dartins' hallway when I went out with Frankie. Toby's dad was looking uncomfortable. 'It's just that—'

'Don't you worry, Red,' my mother said soothingly, putting her hand on his arm. 'You can have anything you need. You know my sister Belle, I think? Of course. Now, you'd like our Mia to help?'

'If it's not too much trouble.' Toby's dad breathed a sigh of relief. 'Frankie and I are going up to the site, to the incident headquarters. The police are up there already. They've been at it since first light, and it appears there have been developments.'

My mother clasped our baby closer, looking shocked. Aunty Belle gasped and put her arm around Mum's shoulders, and Lucky Day wailed, no doubt catching Mum's mood.

With my heart hammering, I stepped down from the porch and whispered, 'Developments?'

Toby's dad nodded, clasping his hands together in front of him. 'Yes. No sign of Toby or … or the kidnapper—Vin will have told you all about her, Anna. The police think there's an off-chance she might be making her way back here, that her next target may be our home. We're not really sure what she wants, but the police believe there's a slight possibility she'll bring Toby here, and ask for ransom or something. I'd very much like Mia to stay with Helen, if that's all right.'

'Of course!' answered my mother. 'Much more important than school. But, Red, why do you have to go to the mountain? If they are not there anymore, if they have disappeared?'

'Ah,' Toby's dad said, again taking his time. He licked his lips and swallowed before speaking. 'Ah, well, that's the not-so-good development, Anna. They want me to identify something, some personal property that might belong to Toby.'

'Oh no!' Aunty Belle wailed dramatically, and then immediately tried to pretend she wasn't thinking the worst. 'I mean, of course, that doesn't mean anything. Personal property—could be anything. Could be nothing. I mean, I mean, well, you know.'

'Yes, yes, of course,' Toby's dad said automatically. 'Probably nothing. All the same, I must go, and Frankie's going to come with me.'

'What about the policeman, you know, the police communication person? The one who went home with you?' I asked.

'Oh, him,' said Toby's dad. 'Yes, he's at home too, so you'll
be quite safe. I just don't like the thought of Helen being there
all alone, worrying about everything. I'd feel much better if you
would keep her company, Mia. I promise you, Anna, the girls
will be safe there.'

'Can I, Mum? Can I go?'

'Yes, darling, I already said so. Go get dressed. I'll send her
straight over, Red, don't worry.'

'Thanks! Hope I haven't kept anyone late?'

Both Mum and Aunty Belle protested that of course they
would still be on time, though anyone could see that they and
the boys were all going to be late. It didn't really matter. What
was important was helping Helen to wait out the morning. And
doing anything I could to help get Toby back, even if it meant
standing up to a vengeful monster on our neighbour's doorstep.
I waved a hasty farewell to Toby's dad and dashed back into the
house to get out of my PJs and into my jeans.

CHAPTER 23

HELEN AND RAIN HAVE AN IDEA

Helen let me in the front door and clutched me in an enormous hug. After a moment, I pulled back so I could see her face. She looked terrible, her eyes all red and swollen with crying, and a really shaky smile on her mouth.

'Oh, Helen!' I said, which was all I could think of. We hugged again, and then she took me through the lounge room and into the kitchen.

'Have you had any breakfast? I'm about to do some crumpets and honey.'

'That sounds great,' I told her. 'Can I help?'

'Of course. Why don't you make us some tea? And could you ask Constable Maric if he wants anything? He's up in Toby's room.'

I switched the kettle on and started out to find the policeman, and then I realised what she'd said. 'They're in Toby's room? What do they want in there? He hates anyone poking around in there!'

'I know.' Helen sighed. 'The police think they can learn all about Tobes by looking at his things. I told them nothing's changed in there since Mum left, but they still want to look. It's procedure, which is a sacred word, apparently.'

'But this, this horrible Mussari woman, she's got nothing to do with anything in Toby's room!'

Helen shrugged. 'I've tried to tell them, and so has Dad. They think maybe she contacted him before, or something like that. They think she might have been watching him the last few weeks since she got out of prison. Dad hopes that Inspector Gray can sort it out for us. Anyway,' she finished with a brittle smile, 'Toby will be home soon and they can all go away.'

'Of course. As far away as they possibly can. Off the edge of the earth, with Orsa Mussari first.' I felt worse than ever at the helpless, hopeful look on Helen's face, but I knew I was there to make her feel better, so I did my best to return her smile. 'I'll be right back.'

Constable Maric was a balding, middle-aged man with a flat, pale face and small, dark eyes. He looked as if he's never moved faster than a tortoise, and I soon found out he had an annoying habit of nodding at any word anyone said to him. If one of those bobble-toys people have in the back windows of their cars was brought to life and stuck in a police uniform, that's exactly what Constable Maric would look like.

I found him sitting on Toby's bed, his hands clasped between his knees, looking at the floor.

'Constable Maric?'

He looked up and nodded at me, the first of many times.

'Would you like a tea, or coffee, or anything to eat?' As I spoke, I stepped right up to the doorway. From there, I could see Toby's room was a complete mess, with everything moved from its usual place, doors and drawers open, laptop missing from the desk, books pulled off the shelves, and even the bedclothes stripped from the mattress.

My mouth dropped open again. I couldn't ignore this, this

destruction of Toby's place. 'What have you done? Why did you make all this mess? Why have you wrecked Toby's room?'

The policeman bobbed his head. 'All under control, miss. Coffee would be lovely.'

'But why? How could you do that? What on earth are you looking for?'

He did the bobble-doll nod again. Already, it was seriously annoying. 'We're just looking for any little clues, miss, that's all. You never know what bit of information might help.'

Just then, a pitiful wailing started from right under where the policeman was sitting. He nodded more emphatically.

'There it goes again. Seems your Toby's got a pet cat. Lives under the bed. That's the one thing I haven't been able to get at.' As he spoke, he held one hand out toward me, displaying a neat collection of scratches all over the back of it. 'It's a smelly little thing, I must say. But I've called in the blokes from the pound, the dog catchers. Cat catchers, I guess. They'll sort it out for me. Just waiting for them now.'

I had a very, very bad feeling about that. Frankie had told me all about the little cat family that Toby had rescued, and there was no way I was going to let this lumbering bobble-doll have them taken to the pound by some nasty cat catcher. Toby wouldn't want them stuck in a cage in the lost dogs home. I'm not especially good with animals, because we've never had any pets, but yesterday Katkin trusted me enough to ride on my knee, and that gave me confidence.

'Listen,' I said, 'how about you go down for your coffee, and I'll see if I can move the cat? Then you can look under the bed as much as you want.'

Constable Maric considered this, swaying his head back and forth, looking over my head at the wall. 'Fair enough,' he said at last. 'Just don't touch anything else, right, miss? I need to check everything that Toby has in here. Everything. So you're only to move that cat, right? Don't touch anything else.'

I let out the breath I was holding. I realised I felt quite worried for Toby's cat family, and that I really, really didn't want the police or the catchers from the pound to get their hands on them.

'Right. You go downstairs, Constable, and I'll see what I can do.' I put on my good student smile, and it seemed to work.

The policeman was slow getting to his feet, and he took a long, careful look around the room before he left, as if he was taking a mental picture of exactly where everything was in case I was tempted to touch something without permission. And, of course, he nodded to me as he went past.

As soon as he was gone, I knelt down next to Toby's bed and peered underneath. A small black-and-white cat was sitting up on its haunches, both paws raised in defence, its mouth open in a snarl. When it saw me, it drew breath audibly. It had to be the little mother cat Frankie told me about. I thought she was about to attack me, but instead she blinked and let out a long sigh, followed by a pathetic *meow*.

'What's the matter, kitty?' I asked her. 'Has the nasty man been mean to you?'

The cat just blinked again, settling back into the cat basket pushed under Toby's mattress. A few little squeaks and a bit of shuffling let me know the kittens were all there, too.

That, and the pretty revolting smell of cat urine. And of sweaty sports clothes. It looked like someone (or some cat) had turned Toby's washing basket upside down and then pulled every piece of dirty clothing into the cat-bed for the kittens to lie on. And to pee on, and anything else they needed to do, judging by the smell. Ugh. Worse than August and Joseph before bath time.

The little mother cat grabbed my attention back with

another pathetic *meow*, this time making a bigger note of protest, as if demanding that I do something about this horrid predicament.

I sat back on my heels and looked around the chaos of Toby's room. Sure enough, the police had moved every single item without thought or reason. There was the food and drink for the cats—stupidly, halfway across the room, placed on top of Toby's desk. As if they could reach it there! And, even more stupidly, the kitty litter-tray had been pushed out into the hall. Constable Maric had no sense of what this little cat needed. She was probably hungry, thirsty, and terrified of him, not to mention having a bladder about to burst.

I bent down again, gently reaching my hand under the bed. The cat and I both watched wide-eyed as my fingers touched the side of the cat basket. As I slowly brought the other hand under the bed in the same way, I felt something bump my elbow aside. To my surprise, it was the Dartins' real cat, I mean, the one they've always had—the big, handsome Maine Coon with the champagne-coloured coat. Flax.

Flax pushed in alongside my outreached arm and started quite a conversation with the little mother, with meows going back and forth like a verse and chorus. In a very short time, all the mother cat's fear collapsed and she let me drag the smelly basket out into the open. She didn't even protest when I gathered the basket, cat, kittens, Toby's now extremely dirty school shirt and all, into my arms.

Flax stalked out from under Toby's bed, tail high in the air, and went ahead of us out of the room. He led the way downstairs without looking back once and trotted through to the kitchen. There he sent a long, dismissive look at Constable Maric seated at the kitchen table, before he sat down near the stove and began to groom his spotless fur. When I stood in the doorway, my armful of cat-dom beginning to squeak and complain, Flax looked up at me as if to say, 'Well, put them down here. What are you waiting for?' So I did just that, and he actually leaned over and licked the back of my wrist.

In no time at all, Helen arranged everything for them, even shaking out the dirty washing from the bottom of the cat basket and handing it, with a formal smile, in one smelly bundle to Constable Maric.

'I suppose you want to look through this as well,' she said.

When everyone was clean and fed and comfortable again, and the policeman had taken the bundle of dirty clothes back up to Toby's room, Helen and I finally sat down to tea and crumpets. I felt much better with all the cats in the room. It was as if I'd rescued them myself, and I liked how Flax was purring, like a steam engine. The kittens were all curled up asleep.

'What's going to happen to them?' I asked.

'Oh, we're keeping them,' said Helen. 'We're going to adopt them. Maggie thinks they're abandoned, so they might even become domesticated again. They're not completely feral, so they'll probably be happy to live with us.'

'Poor things. They're lucky Toby found them.'

'Mmm. I've been thinking about that. You know what? I bet Orsa planted those cats deliberately.'

'Deliberately? What do you mean?'

'Inspector Gray said she's been out of prison for some months. He's pretty sure she's been watching us, watching Toby, trying to find out if we ever see Mum. For someone with Orsa Mussari's abilities, it wouldn't take much to work out that Toby has cat magic.'

'Oh, yes, I see.' I swallowed. Orsa was so terrifying that the thought of her watching us made me shiver. Now that Helen had mentioned magic, I felt I could ask her more. 'You know, Helen, this, um, this magic business. Can you tell me more about it? I only heard about it, I mean I only realised, yesterday. Frankie explained a bit, while we were chasing that bus.'

Just then the back door opened, and Professor Dartin walked in. He looked more refreshed than he was at the hospital yesterday, dressed in a smart dark suit and smelling of fresh aftershave, but he had a deep frown on his face.

'Helen!' he said loudly. 'And Mia, isn't it? Any news? Are the police still here?'

'Constable Maric is upstairs, searching through Toby's dirty washing,' said Helen. 'Do you want tea, Uncle Rain?'

'Yes, thanks.' He took a chair on the other side of the table. 'Dirty washing?' He tutted, dismissing it as unimportant. 'I've come to talk to you, Helen. I can't get on to your father, and I've had an idea.'

Helen sat beside me. 'I hope it's a good one. I was just about to explain to Mia the complications of the magic part of our family.'

'Oh! Right, go ahead. The more she understands, the better. Is this crumpet for me?' Professor Dartin hunted around for butter and honey while Helen continued our conversation.

'I'm sorry we haven't talked about this before,' she said.

I shrugged. 'That's okay. I don't want to pry.'

Helen squeezed my hand. 'It's not especially secret. It's not dangerous or anything. It's not even particularly useful! More of a burden, really.'

'A burden? Oh, you mean if you can see what other people can't, but you can't explain?'

'Sometimes.' Helen nodded. 'And sometimes it means you have to do things you don't want to do, because you know it's the right thing.' She sighed. 'My parents, and Uncle Rain here, they've always gone out of their way to help other people, to do what's right. They don't always succeed, of course, but they have to try.'

Professor Dartin made a coughing noise, looking away as if he couldn't hear what his niece was saying.

'You too, I guess?' I asked her.

Helen smiled. 'I hope so. The law, for me, is about doing what's right. I think I will be stuck with a very small and very poor clientele, though, when I go into practice on my own.'

I thought for a minute. 'So, like, can you spot when people tell lies? That sort of thing?'

'Yes, that's part of it for me. And sometimes, seeing that certain people should or shouldn't—no, that's not quite right—that certain people are going to be good or not so good for each other. Not that any amount of magic can stop anyone making bad decisions. Whether you're magic or flat, you can still make mistakes.'

'Huh. And Orsa Mussari?'

'Well, I've been thinking. I wouldn't be surprised if she watched us long enough to learn quite a lot. Like, that Toby is great with cats, for example. I really do think Orsa planted those cats herself. She deliberately dumped them where we'd find them. And Katkin—well, she's a special kind of magic cat, and she's been missing for years and years. I think Orsa had her trapped, and that she used Katkin to catch Toby.'

'Aha!' Professor Dartin said. 'Exactly what I've been thinking! And you know what else?'

We both looked at him. 'The bangle! Don't you remember the bangle Toby talked about? He saw it, and then Katkin jumped out of it?'

Helen nodded. 'Yes, he said it was silver, and had a cat charm, and when he went to pick it up—'

'The charm turned into a cat, right?' the professor finished. 'I think Orsa had that bangle all along. I bet she had Katkin trapped inside. Imagine, hidden in there for years!'

'That sounds awful,' I said. 'Imagine being trapped with her!'

Professor Dartin agreed. 'And I think she probably tried to use Katkin's magic to find Jenny, but that plan went pear-shaped. Jenny's nowhere to be found, no matter what sort of magic Orsa might use. Jenny has her own magic, and she has a huge circle of well-wishers to draw on, including all the people who helped her disappear in the first place.'

'Is that what happened?' I asked. 'Toby's mum disappeared by magic? And you magic people helped her?'

'Not quite the way you think, Mia,' Helen explained. 'Mum disappeared with the help of the magic community, who did small things like cover official traces and confuse official records. That sort of thing. None of us—none of the family—was involved, so no magic trail can lead anyone from us to her. She will be living an ordinary life somewhere. She hasn't vanished into smoke or anything.'

Helen looked sad when she explained all this. It made me feel sad too, but the professor was much more positive.

'Jenny is safe where Orsa will never find her.' He grinned. 'You know what I think? I think Orsa no longer has any connections she can call in. She burned a helluva lot of her bridges chasing Jenny, and even more during the trial. I doubt she has any magic of her own left. She squandered her own tiny gift on selfish things long before she even went to trial, so the only magic she could possibly rely on for this venture was what she borrowed from a magic cat.'

'Oh! So if we get hold of the bangle, the one she used to control Katkin,' I said, 'we can stop her?'

'Yes!' Helen and Professor Dartin said at the same time.

PART SEVEN
TOBY

CHAPTER 24
THE TROUBLE WITH ORSA

'No, no, no!' Orsa kept saying. Her voice was all small and sweet and pathetic, like a lost toddler wanting its mother. 'My bangle, my bangle! Give it back. Give it back, please. Please!'

She made me feel sick. I didn't need Katkin to remind me of who she really was. The last thing I would ever do was give Orsa the silver bangle.

Anyway, the thing was pretty much stuck on my wrist now.

'I don't think I could give it back,' I told her, 'even if I wanted to. And believe me, I don't want to. I want you never to have this in your hands again. It's mine now, and Katkin is safe from you.'

I glanced down at the silver bangle on my wrist. It looked less like a charm bracelet now, and more like a woven chain. The sort of man-bracelet a trendy city guy might wear. Actually, I quite liked the look of it—less shiny, more black, slightly chunky, but not too big.

Also, it didn't look silver anymore—it could have been stainless steel or platinum, or maybe white gold like my dad's wedding ring. I ran a finger over it, surprised that it seemed warm against my cold skin.

Katkin leaped into my arms and nestled her head under my chin. *You can't get it off anyway*, she told me. *You're the rightful owner.*

'*I'm* the rightful owner!' Orsa shrieked. She obviously had enough magic to hear Katkin's mindspeech. 'My grandfather Julio brought that all the way from Sicily. He brought it with him on the boat! It's been in my family for generations, I tell you. It's mine, it's mine, it's mine!'

Katkin hissed, a piercing loudness by my ear. *He stole it! Thief, thief! Thief and murderer, that's what your grandfather was.*

'No!' Orsa cried again. 'He never! That was all a mistake. Nobody was meant to get hurt. If your stupid owner had only handed it over like a sensible woman, he would never have killed her. It's her fault that he needed to kill and steal. This is all her fault, all of it. She was stupid. Everyone knows she was stupid!'

Serena was not my 'owner', said Katkin. I hadn't heard her sweet cat voice so cold; it was as if she suddenly turned into an ancient wise woman, judging souls for their worth. *Serena was my soulmate, like Tobias Felix here, in her time. She was never stupid! She was clever, and loyal, and selfless. And Julio killed her, just to get the bracelet. Just to steal me and my magic.*

Orsa subsided at the little cat's intensity and huddled against one of the standing rocks, sobbing miserably. She was muttering the word 'stupid' over and over, as if that would remake the past into the way she wanted it to be.

Katkin buried her head in my neck and was doing a bit of muttering herself, though I couldn't quite catch what she was saying. I looked around, wishing I could see more. Apart from the star-lit expanse of sky silhouetting the enormous rocks above us, the bush was cloaked in its night-time guise of shadows. The rain had petered out, but a chill mist was thickening by the minute. Even if the moon were full and bright, that mountain mist would stop me from seeing my way out of here.

I bent down till I could touch noses with Katkin. 'I think we're stuck here for the night,' I said to the little cat, 'unless you know a magic way to light up the path?'

Katkin shuddered, lifting her gaze to search the dense bush around us, digging her claws a little deeper into my skin. I could see starlight reflected in her eyes, a kind of green sparkle. She turned her head up and blinked slowly at me.

You don't know the way home, Tobias Felix? she asked me. *Really?*

I sighed. 'Not in the dark, no. We're way off the regular trails. I could make a guess, but it's dangerous to go blundering around on a mountainside in the dark.'

Katkin's claws dug deeper. *I'm cold. Can I get inside your jacket?*

'Sure. In fact, why don't we go into the cave? We may as well make the best of the shelter.'

I stood up and looked at the dejected huddle that was Orsa, still sobbing her heart out, though the sobs were weak and fractured and petulant, like a child determined to keep crying until its parents gave in to its wants. While I would have been more than happy to see her disappear off the face of the earth, I wasn't so sure I wanted her to freeze to death just a few steps from me.

'Orsa? Why don't you come into the cave? It's going to be icy here before long.'

'Leave me alone! Shut up and go away!'

Charming. 'As you wish.'

Still holding Katkin close, I ducked down to find my way between the leaning rocks. It was surprisingly dry inside, with the rocks forming a complete roof overhead, one that I knew was covered with those scrubby bushes and hanging vines. An even bigger surprise was that I could see my way pretty well. The silver bangle glowed softly on my wrist. It wasn't enough light to read by, but it certainly helped me to check for spiders, snakes, scorpions, or any other nasties. Strangely, there was no sign of any animal habitation: no owl pellets or bat droppings, and no cobwebs, which seemed pretty odd, given that this seemed to be quite a safe den for any bush creature who wanted dry, warm, secure shelter.

Katkin nudged my chin, telling me to look up. Expecting that she'd spotted a tarantula about to drop on my head, I tensed as I lifted my eyes to scan the ceiling.

Then I gasped.

A wide swathe of the cave's roof had been painted over. From one side of the cave to the other, the flapping wings of black crows stood out against a sweep of ochre paint, like a river of birds flying toward the sunset.

It was the most beautiful thing I'd ever seen. Words weren't enough. I could only say 'Wow!', and I said it quite a few times.

This is the cave of crows, Katkin told me. *Orsa can't come in, not without the bangle. The magic here is too strong.*

'And too pure,' I guessed, feeling something like a pause all around me, as if the cave itself was holding its breath while it studied me. 'What about us?' I asked the little cat. 'Somehow I don't feel that I deserve to be here, to see this.'

Katkin draped herself across my shoulders. *We can stay, but only for a little while. The crows will accept us, just for a bit. But you should look as much as you want now, because we'll probably never see this again.*

A once in a lifetime opportunity, then.

I settled onto my heels and sat with my back against the rock near the entry. I could see that the glorious sweep of birds led from this entrance across to the other side of the cavern, almost as if it was pointing to a way out, the only way out. But as far as I could see, there was no gap in the rocks on the far side. Whatever path led out of here to the west, it wasn't for us. That path was one we could never take.

We sat there for a long time, Katkin purring like a small engine as she snuggled into my collar. Even being able to look at the painting was amazing, although I knew somehow that it wasn't my place, or my destiny, to follow the birds' path. The crow road was not for me; somebody else's magic. It was like I was allowed to rest on a bench in a private garden, but only for a little while before I would be ushered out and the gate closed behind me.

Slowly, I let my eyes rest on every single painted crow that made its way across the ceiling. Each one was different, and the longer I looked, the more individual features I could see, as my eyes adjusted to the low light. I detected details in the ochre background. Many other animals were there, lightly present in a graceful deepening of colour, or delicately sketched in outline. They were hard to see at first because, for one thing, they were subtly drawn, but mostly because of the perspective. Kangaroos, emus, snakes, turtles, lizards—they were all there, but weirdly, I was seeing them from overhead, kind of like the view you'd get from a plane. The whole painting showed the other animals looking up from the ground at the flock of crows overhead, as if the painter was looking down from above the crows. I could have looked at it all night.

My kidnapper was just outside, and eventually I realised she was still crying, a shivering sort of sound that broke into my wonder about the cave. We were dry and sheltered, but out there an icy wind was stirring the mist. I shrugged out of my jacket and handed it through the entry, merely calling Orsa's name, and then scooted back inside. As Katkin and I settled in to wait through the dark hours, I saw a brief glimmer overhead on the roof of the cave, as if the crows were now flying through a skein of stars. Then the light from the bangle on my wrist gently faded, tucking the darkness around us like a blanket.

Tired, hungry, and lost; somehow none of it mattered. We were together and nobody could ever pull us away from each other.

We fell asleep.

CHAPTER 25
THE WAY HOME

FRIDAY

I woke to the sound of birdsong. A very cheerful kookaburra was announcing the new day with a bundle of enthusiasm, as if there had never been such a morning before. Maybe there never had been.

Katkin stood up from where she curled on my chest all night and stretched, making a high arch of her back and then thoroughly shaking her whole body. She sneezed twice, her little claws clutching me with each gasp and blow. It made me laugh, just a bit. I could have sworn she gave me an answering grin.

She jumped off and headed out, no doubt hurrying to make use of the bush as a bathroom facility. I needed to do the same, so I got up to follow her. I was stiff and aching in every muscle, and there was old blood crusted all over my face. My mouth tasted awful. I was very thirsty, and I needed water for a wash, too.

As I hunkered down to leave through the cave's low entrance, I looked up at the roof, but I couldn't see anything. The whole ceiling was lost in deep shadows. The roof also seemed to be much higher than last night, completely out of reach, too far even for my eyes to see. I smiled up at it anyway and crouched low to get out.

It was only when I had walked halfway around the standing rocks of Babylon, and I was scooping up icy water from the tinkling little rivulet on the far side of the formation, that I suddenly realised Orsa wasn't there. I lapped up a couple of handfuls and rubbed my wet palms over my face, which made me feel a bit better. Then I went back and searched the trampled space by the cavern entrance, where Orsa had huddled in my jacket the night before.

There was no sign of her. No jacket either.

Oh well. Although it was still cold, there were some high, soft clouds visible through the treetops. No mist and no rain, and not the slightest breath of wind. Knowing that the breeze would probably pick up later when the sun came up behind those clouds, I decided it was better to try finding our way down the mountain than to go chasing after Orsa. I didn't want to be lost in the bush any longer. And really, Orsa was a problem for the police now, not for me. She'd done her worst. Now that I had the bangle safely on my wrist, it looked like Orsa had no access to magic. I only hoped nobody had been badly injured, or even killed, by her crazy rampage through the city. I tried not to imagine too much. I could find out soon enough, if I could get myself back to civilisation.

Katkin was sitting tidily at my feet, the picture of a domestic cat waiting to be fed. I smiled down at her. 'Hungry, are you? So am I.'

Let's go home. Can you find the way now?

'Well, I hope we can retrace the way we came.'

Katkin gave me that superior cat look. *Hope? Retrace?* She put on a cattish grin. *Just get us home.*

Oh. She clearly expected me to use magic to find our way, but I wasn't sure I could do that. 'I don't think—' I began.

You didn't think you could resist Orsa in the hut either. Katkin licked one paw as if she hadn't a worry in the world beyond repairing her appearance. After all our adventures, I had to admit she was looking a little bedraggled, a condition that obviously needed all her attention.

I sighed. It was useless to protest. I'd always known there was never any point in arguing with a cat, especially a magic cat. Cats know everything—just ask them. Look at Flax! He was the most knowing inhabitant of our entire household, no matter how many professors and surgeons and lawyers we had in the family. The thought of Flax made me smile, and then I felt the hairs along my spine stand up, singly and in sequence, like a row of soldiers coming to attention. *Flax*, I thought, closing my eyes. *Home. Where are you?*

A minute, or maybe longer, and I opened my eyes again to find I had my hands clasped tightly together in front of my heart. Katkin was seated neatly in front of me, her tail tucked around her feet, her head on one side as she looked up at my face. If a cat could ever be said to smile kindly rather than give that sardonic grin, then Katkin was definitely smiling kindly.

Well, Tobias Felix? Which way?

'Want to be carried?' I responded.

The little cat leaped into my arms, draping herself comfortably across my shoulder. *I'll walk when we get to a proper path,* she told me. *No sense in us both getting covered in burrs and cobwebs.*

I laughed. 'True.'

Finding the way was now just as easy as using a GPS; 'home' was right there in my senses. Even when I had to step off the direct route to skirt a patch of blackberry or to scramble across a rocky slope, my sense of direction never wavered. We began gradually making our way down and across a moderate incline, and in hardly any time at all, I lost sight of the place where we'd stayed overnight. It was like I imagined the whole thing: Babylon Rock and the cave of painted crows, the dark hours of safety, the magic bracelet, Orsa whining and complaining.

But I hadn't imagined it. I had a magic cat curled around my neck, doing a pretty good impression of a winter scarf.

Katkin spent most of the time looking over my shoulder, studying the bush behind us. She was so intent on this that after a while, I got a niggle of worry.

'Is Orsa still out there, do you think?'

No, she's nowhere near.

'Good.' I trekked another hundred metres or so. Sunlight slanted through the canopy, making it easier for me to see my footing. Still, Katkin was preoccupied, and I kept worrying about it. She seemed in a strange mood, and although I was good at reading cat body language, I couldn't actually tell what they were thinking. I wondered whether Katkin was grieving for Serena, the person Orsa's grandfather Julio killed, or if she was just exhausted from her ordeal with the magic bracelet. Maybe it would help to talk.

'Katkin? Are you okay? You're very quiet.'

She snuggled against my neck. *Just thinking.* I felt a rush of warm air as she let out a sigh. *Not happy thoughts.*

'Anything wrong?'

Nothing, she assured me. *Just remembering what that repulsive creature said.*

'Orsa? Don't give her another thought. Sounds like her whole family would do anything to get rich and powerful. Robbery, murder, kidnapping! They sound horrible. Let's forget about them.'

Yes, the cat said in a quiet voice. *But in a way, I suppose it was stupid, you know, what Serena did.*

Ah. 'How about I sit down and rest for a few minutes? Maybe you'd like to tell me about it?'

Katkin's claws stabbed me for a moment as she tensed and then relaxed. *Yes. You should know.*

I was very sore and tired myself, so I was quite happy to have a rest. I looked around for a good place to sit. We'd climbed down into the bush below the tree line, so I thought we couldn't be all that far from the hut by the waterfall. In fact, I could faintly hear water somewhere below us. That made me feel safe and so close to help and home that I didn't see any desperate need to hurry. We would lose our privacy soon enough when we got back to civilisation. Talking this problem through with Katkin for a few minutes was more important. Besides, I was curious about Serena, and how her relationship with Katkin worked.

I sat down on a mossy rock at the base of a tree fern, where one shaft of sunlight gave me the tiniest bit of warmth in the chilly morning air, even though I knew I would be sitting down on a wet surface. Everything in the surrounding bush was wet, but because we were both still damp from our adventures in yesterday's rain, sitting on the wet ground wasn't going to make things much worse. I cuddled Katkin close on my lap, one arm around her to keep her as warm as could be. She leaned back against me, staring at the way we had come, her head tilted to my chest.

'Talk to me, then,' I said. 'Just tell me everything you want me to know. I'm listening.'

Serena. She was wonderful and brave. But it was war, you see. We were helping people to hide, and to escape if we could. We helped magic people and flat people—it didn't matter. Then Serena realised that a woman with a cat by her side all the time was too obvious. We became too identifiable, too easy to find, and we had too many narrow escapes. So Serena decided she had to hide me, too.

I guessed, from all the clues Orsa let out, that she was talking about World War Two. Orsa Mussari said her grandfather came to Australia on the boat. That would have been last century, in the forties or fifties, when Australia had that big migration from Italy and Greece. We covered all that in Culture & Society class a couple of years ago.

Serena, whoever she was, sounded like a resistance fighter of some sort, definitely someone who wanted to protect people from being persecuted. She was probably trying to help Jewish people to hide from the Nazis. That was very, very dangerous and no way could she afford to be caught, or even to be noticed.

'I think I understand,' I told Katkin. 'Serena made the bracelet as a magic place for you to hide?'

Yes. And it worked well. Before that, I always had to find a hiding spot for myself, or let Serena go ahead alone and meet her somewhere. But there were other people who knew about the bracelet, who knew about the magic. Even people who innocently told others that a woman with a cat might be able to help them. Of course, those others told others, and eventually the wrong people heard about it.

'You were betrayed?' The old story of war: there was always someone who'd betray your secrets to the enemy, no matter how much good you might be doing. Desperation made people vulnerable to evil.

Yes, Katkin said again. *When the wrong people heard about it, we had to run. We ran all the way down the boot of Italy. Then everything went wrong. More wrong than it already was.*

Katkin was quiet for so long this time that I took up the story, which now seemed so obvious to me. 'So you got to Sicily, hoping for sanctuary, or hoping to escape, and Orsa's grandfather found you. He killed Serena and took the bracelet.'

Katkin let out a long sigh. *It's true that he only intended to steal it,* she admitted. *He didn't know about the magic Serena had created, how the bracelet was tuned to just one person. Julio Mussari was a flat, you see. A greedy, selfish, violent man, but flat as can be.*

'Do you mean that until he stole a magic cat inside that bracelet, the Mussari family had no magic?'

No, his wife was magic, and powerful. She did things, made the bracelet fit his wrist. She was ... she was strong. Katkin shuddered.

'Things? Like torture, you mean?' I was thinking of the half-healed wound on Katkin's side, the one Maggie had dressed for her.

Katkin stood up in my lap. She butted her head at my chin. *Enough. Now you know. You know why I'm so glad I found you.*

'Me too.' I swallowed all my other questions about Serena and Julio, all my outrage. The little cat was right: enough was enough. 'Just one more question, then. Do you want me to destroy this thing?' I had in mind Gollum and the One Ring, and how Frodo had to throw it into the molten lava in *Lord of the Rings.*

No. No, better not. We may need it someday. It's not a bad idea, in the right hands.

'Fine.'

Anyway, Katkin said with a typically practical turn of mind, *you wouldn't be able to. Whatever you did, you couldn't make every piece of magic silver disappear. Even in silver dust, it would remember its power.*

'I see.' That was enough to know. It was up to me to be the guardian of this particular piece of magic. 'Come on, I think we're near the actual path. Soon I won't have to carry you, little one.'

And me so heavy, Tobias Felix, said Katkin. Her tone was comical, but she had a wistful look on her face. I took her in my arms again and we began the last trek out of the bush.

In a few minutes, I was positive that the sounds of water

had exactly the same pattern I heard from the waterfall the day before. With any luck, the police or the Search and Rescue team would still have someone posted there, just in case we reappeared. Or they might even be organising a new search from that very point, taking up where they left off the day before—where I left them, I guess. I was quite looking forward to seeing those officers Orsa attacked, hoping with all my heart that they suffered no ill-effects. I wanted to see them well and working again. I wanted to see that warm smile from Sergeant Miller.

But when I went round the next corner and pushed another scratchy, dripping branch of tea tree out of my way, I came face to face with someone—*something?*—I never thought to see again.

The kangaroo-rat driver was waiting for me on the path.

I stood with my mouth open in shock for a moment or two. The last I saw, he was scampering across the road with an ungainly kind of hoppity-stagger-jump, his powerful roo hindquarters bursting through the shreds of his uniform. Now I saw something had gone horribly wrong with whatever transformation Orsa put on him.

He was covered partly with reddish kangaroo fur, but mostly with wrinkled pale skin that shone like scar tissue. His shoulders were bent horribly into a hunchback shape, and his face was all wrong—broad human forehead above a sticking-out marsupial jaw, his mouth lined with dozens of miniature herbivore teeth. His fur-covered, human-style ears looked like they'd been stuck sideways on his head by an imaginative toddler. His eyes were enormous and set so wide apart that he had to turn his head to one side or the other just to look at me. His little arms ended in misshapen hands with not enough fingers. His whole body was shaking so much it was a wonder he could stay upright at all.

I stared at him and he shuffled uneasily from side to side,

moving his weight from one huge hind foot to the other, while his ridiculous hands made tiny circles in front of his chest. Katkin clawed her way up to stand on my shoulder, her back arched as she hissed fiercely, too close to my ear.

Oh! she said when she got a good look at him. She settled down, her claws unlatching from my skin. *That's not good.*

I glanced sideways at her to see if she had any suggestions, but she was tilting her head with simple curiosity as she gazed at the creature blocking our way.

'What can we do?'

That got her attention. *Do? You want to help this thing?*

I squirmed under her accusing look. 'Um, I don't know, maybe? He looks pretty harmless.'

Harmless? He's one of hers. Rotten to the heart!

As if he understood Katkin's words, the sorry creature put back his head and let out a ragged cry, like the sound you'd expect from a distressed donkey. Half-bray, half-cough, and totally pathetic.

I don't trust him.

'Maybe she just made use of him. Maybe he's just an ordinary creature that she caught and twisted into ... into ... whatever that is.'

Katkin lifted a lip. *He's one of hers. He must be.*

'I'm not so sure.' Perhaps it was his huge brown eyes that made me feel so bad about him. I'd always been a sucker for dogs, and this bloke looked as wretched as an abandoned puppy.

Huh. Katkin leaned forward, her whiskers twitching as she sought out the creature's scent. She relaxed a little. *Tobias Felix, you have good instincts.*

'So you think he's okay? He's not evil?'

I think he's too stupid to be evil. Not that I trust stupid.

'I feel sorry for him.'

Katkin sighed. *Of course you do. Go on, see if you can help.*

'I don't even know how to start.'

Katkin glared at me a moment before she leaped lightly off my shoulder to sit on the side of the narrow path. She then lifted a paw and began licking it, as if the whole incident had nothing to do with her. The kangaroo-rat thing whimpered, a heart-breaking sound that set my teeth on edge.

I had no idea what to do, but I started by looking closely at him, trying to figure out what he was before Orsa got hold of him. I did a kind of running commentary that he tried to follow, and while I scanned him from the top of his misshapen head to the thin scabby tail that just touched the ground behind his legs, his breathing slowed and his whimpers quietened.

'So, you look like a marsupial to me, really. You're very big, but you seem to be more kangaroo-rat than kangaroo. Why do I think that, I wonder? Maybe it's your eyes. Really large, you know? No whites showing, just huge and brown and shiny. And your paws are quite small for the rest of you. And you're a bit bent over, like you'd prefer to scamper along the ground. You can jump, but you can run too, can't you? Yes, I think you're actually a little, teeny, tiny, kangaroo-rat, with a long thin tail and a small head, and smooth brown fur. That's what you should be. Just an ordinary little—Oh, wow!'

I stepped back and stood amazed as the creature wriggled and squirmed, telescoping down to its proper size as I waffled on, a bit like Orsa shrank when she lost her grip on anger. My talking seemed to soothe it.

'That's better,' I said softly. 'Now you just keep thinking teeny-tiny kangaroo-rat thoughts, and you'll stay that way.'

I didn't actually know if that was true, but the creature fixed me with one large eye and blinked rapidly, like he was trying not to cry. I had to blink myself. 'Go on then, off you go. No more magic for you. Kangaroo-rat thoughts, right?'

Away he scampered. I sat down abruptly on the path, suddenly exhausted, and Katkin jumped into my lap.

Good work, she said.

'I didn't do anything.'

Cats can laugh, even magic cats.

You're so funny, Tobias Felix. You saw him. You listened to him. You found what he really is. That's magic, you know. Not everyone can do that.

It sounded fanciful to me, but I thought of it this way. The poor creature had a lot of magic floating around his body, from when Orsa had him under control, only he didn't know what to shape himself back into. I just put his thoughts into words for him.

Magic? Maybe.

Katkin looked at me, her head tilted to one side. I had to smile at her.

'Whatever. Let's get going.'

She led the way, her tail high as she tripped down the track until the next overgrown bit, when she demanded to be carried again. We continued on.

After a while, we rounded a sharp bend, and I saw another wallaby trail leading off from the main track, going about twenty metres down through the scrub to the properly formed Parks path. We had come out right above the wooden tourist hut that looked out onto the running water. The whole area was crowded with variously uniformed people milling about. It looked kind of like busloads of high school students had come to the same spot for a sports carnival and needed to figure out what to do next.

I couldn't hear anything they said because of the water crashing on the rocks. I couldn't wait to see their faces when I scrambled down to meet them. I had to admit I was cheered that there were so many of them down there, all trying to find me, especially after I'd been so unreasonable, in their eyes I guessed, in running off after they first found me. Yet here they all were again. The relief I felt at getting back to ordinary people made me warm and cheerful in an instant.

Katkin seemed to catch my mood and wriggled to get free. *I can walk from here*, she told me, bounding out of my arms.

'Sure,' I said, already tackling the slippery way down to the path. A half-dozen rescue staff mustered at the front of the hut, along with a couple of police officers and two men in suits.

One of the suit guys was my dad.

Dad and the other man were bent over what looked like my jacket, and even from a distance, I could see it was filthy with blood. Just my poor nose, I guessed, but to them it must have looked appalling. The other man had one hand on my dad's shoulder.

I clambered down to the path and staggered as quickly as I could around the hut, calling loudly for Dad. I blundered straight into his arms.

As he hugged me tight, I could hear Frankie yelling, 'He's here! He's here! He's alive!'

PART EIGHT
MIA

CHAPTER 26
ORSA'S NEXT PLOY

Helen and her Uncle Rain decided that the best plan for retrieving the magic bangle was to make our way up to incident headquarters, the police caravan on Mountain Road, and let them know that a family heirloom was also missing. I had no idea how they were going to tell the police officers how important it was without mentioning the fact that it was magic, but I was ready to do whatever was needed to get Toby back, so any plan sounded good to me.

'After all,' said Helen, 'it's important information. The mountain is where the trail starts, and the bangle is the best clue to finding Toby. So we have to let all the searchers know how important that bangle is, that it has a sort of connection with Tobes. If they get a sighting of Orsa and Toby, they need to grab her first and get that bangle off her. Then Toby will be out of danger.'

'Yes,' said Professor Dartin. 'I'm certain that without the bangle, she'll have no way to torment us any longer. She won't be able to chase Toby, or imprison Katkin again, or throw cats around as bait. Or trace Jenny, of course, but nothing can do that.'

"

I bit my lip. 'But what can we say? That it's got magic in it?'

'We'll say something,' said Helen. 'I'm a lawyer. I'll think of some good words on the way.'

Professor Dartin waved a hand as though explaining the problem to official staff was a minor matter. 'It makes no difference what they think. No matter what happens, we must get that bangle.'

WARE! WARE! WARE!

The words exploded in my head, louder than how August yelled when he ambushed Joseph from the top bunk. I put my hands up over my ears, but the warning scream kept bursting into my brain.

Helen gave a yip of pure fear, and then yelled, 'Flax! What is it?' at the same time as someone started pounding viciously on the front door.

Constable Maric came thumping down the stairs, releasing his gun from its holster. It was the only time I saw him move faster than a turtle.

'Keep back!' he said sternly, nodding his head and motioning with one hand, as if he was ordering us to retreat into the kitchen. We didn't go.

Then the Dartins' big cat Flax, his fur standing on end, tore right past the policeman and plonked himself in the hallway, standing on his back legs with his forepaws raised, snarling and wailing like a super-powered siren. He looked at least twice as big as usual, and a whole lot more dangerous.

'We're staying with you, Constable,' Professor Dartin snapped in a matter-of-fact voice, as if he wasn't having any arguments about it. 'Nobody is hiding in the kitchen.'

So we three shadowed the policeman to stand near the front door. Helen pushed her way through us and put one hand on the latch. The door shook on its hinges from the force of the hammering. Professor Dartin sidled up to one of the glass panels that framed the doorway and slid a finger neatly behind the curtain.

'It is Orsa Mussari,' he murmured. 'She's alone. No Toby to be seen.' He chewed on his bottom lip and turned to us. 'At least she doesn't seem to be armed.'

'Okay,' Constable Maric said in a loud stage whisper, nodding at each of us in turn. 'Everybody stay calm.'

We looked at each other, all of us pretty steady even though we were on high alert. As far as I could tell, it was Constable Maric who was acting twitchy. I don't think he expected his family liaison duties to include protecting us from home invasion. It seemed a long way from sorting through dirty laundry for clues.

'We're all calm,' said Professor Dartin, as cool as if he was telling us it was a nice day. 'What do you suggest now, Constable?'

The policeman nodded at him. 'That's good. Now we just stay calm. I can put in a call and get help here in no time. While I do that, see if you can stall her for a while. Miss, why don't you ask what she wants and keep her talking?'

Helen narrowed her eyes at the door and called out clearly, 'Who is it?'

Constable Maric stepped back toward the stairs, muttering into his comms unit, his eyes still on the door. There was a buzz of beeping and static, and I heard the words *danger* and *immediate back-up.*

A booming voice made me jump. 'Open the door, girly!' Orsa said in a sing-song tone. 'You'll be so ve-ry sor-ry if you don't!'

'Why should I?' asked Helen. 'Why would I want to let you in?'

'You wanna see your little brother ever again? Ever?' Orsa laughed, a gritty sound that ended in a rumbling cough.

Helen glanced back at the policeman. Constable Maric tiptoed forward, his lips compressed as if he didn't want any sound to escape, or as if he might be sick at any moment. I wasn't reassured. He peeped through the glass panel on the opposite side of the door from where the professor was standing.

He did his stage whisper thing again. 'I can see both her hands, and there's no weapon. Maybe it wouldn't be a bad idea to let her in. You can do the talking, and I can keep her covered,' he offered. 'That way, she can't hurt anyone, and we keep her just where she needs to be. Back-up will be here in an instant, plenty of it. Just let her in to talk and see what she says. She might tell us where young Toby is.'

'Is that safe? You don't think she's dangerous?' asked Professor Dartin.

The policeman shrugged. 'She's one against three, no, four, counting the young miss here, and I have a baton and a gun.'

'True,' said the professor, still spying from the other side of the front door. 'And I wouldn't mind asking her a few questions. She's bound to say too much for her own good.'

'*Let me in!*' Orsa yelled, bashing on the door again, making me jump.

The professor took another long look at her, then turned back to us. There was no need to whisper because she was making such a racket she couldn't possibly hear us.

'Helen, I can't see the bracelet at all. Do you think she might have lost it? Flax, do you feel it?'

He glanced back at the cat, still raised in an attack position, while Constable Maric just frowned in a confused way, like he suspected there was something he wasn't being told. I lifted my eyebrows as though I had no idea what they were talking about either, and the policeman went back to staring at Orsa.

I didn't hear Flax answer, but I saw the professor breathe a sigh of relief.

'That's good news. Excellent news. But do have a care, Helen,' he advised. 'She's dangerous in any state.'

I think Helen understood, like me, that with or without magic, Orsa Mussari was a horrible person who would stop at nothing to get her own way.

Helen put her hand on my shoulder. 'Mia, get behind Flax, if you don't mind,' she said. 'I want both of you to keep a very close eye on our oh-so-charming visitor. Watch very carefully to make sure she doesn't do anything, um, weird with, er, hand gestures and so on.'

Helen wanted me to keep out of danger; I understood that, but I also knew that it was actually quite important to watch Orsa's every move, to make sure she didn't try anything magical. I didn't know what might happen if she summoned that magical mist again, like on the waterfall trail. I went to the spot Helen indicated and watched as she flipped up the latch of the front door. Flax settled back down onto all fours and sat neatly in front of me, motionless as a fluffy toy mascot. I admit I felt safer with him at my feet.

Helen nodded at me and pulled the door open.

Orsa, who'd kept on bashing the door like she was waving enormous drumsticks instead of her bare hands as she was screaming for us to open up, almost fell inside when the door was suddenly yanked away from her. At the same time, there was a huge rush of black wings around the porch. A dozen huge crows flapped around, diving at Orsa's unprotected back. Their cawing sounded really, really loud now that she'd stopped thundering on the door.

'That's the same birds,' I told Helen. 'The crows. The ones that were chasing her, I'm sure of it. They led me and Frankie to the right road yesterday, then flew off into the bush. I bet they went after her.'

'Get them awaaaaay!' Orsa wailed, ducking inside and dropping to her knees while she waved her arms about to protect her head. She looked different from the day before, much smaller and not at all scary. She looked like somebody's eccentric aunty in an old movie: a bit pudgy, old-fashioned, and kind of grubby, like she didn't wash her clothes often enough, or made a habit of sleeping in them. I had to study her hard to make sure it really was her. She didn't seem anywhere near as frightening as when she made those ugly faces at me out the back window of the bus.

As she flopped into the hallway, we all took a half-step backward because it seemed as if the murder of crows was going to invade the house. But even though they looked determined to have a go at Orsa, they weren't quite ready to fly inside. Perhaps they saw Flax leap to his feet, his eyes alight.

Constable Maric went down on one knee, looking stern, and kept his hands braced as he covered Orsa with his weapon. He took absolutely no notice of the noisy, flapping birds mobbing the porch, almost like he couldn't see them.

I heard Professor Dartin coo something under his breath to the birds, something that made them level out their wings and take off into the garden. They set up a kind of observation post in the jacaranda, keeping their beady eyes fixed on us and on the house.

Sudden silence filled the hallway. Everyone took stock.

Then something weird happened. Constable Maric pushed the door shut behind Orsa and got to his feet, turning his gun on us. Orsa scrambled to her feet and grunted. My eyes nearly fell out of my head.

Helen gasped and took a step back. The professor held up both hands.

'Constable,' he said evenly. 'What are you doing?'

'What he should have been doing hours ago,' Orsa growled. 'He owes me!'

'I have no idea what you are talking about,' the professor answered. 'Constable, er, Maric, isn't it? Put that gun down. Now.'

Orsa laughed, looking more like the scary bus conductor again, but the policeman groaned.

'I can't! I have to, you don't understand! It's a family debt. Please, just give her what she wants. Just tell her!'

The professor glared at him, but the policeman kept his pistol levelled, although his hands were shaking as he aimed at Professor Dartin's chest. Helen and I stood uncertainly on either side of him. Nobody said anything for a moment, and the noise of my heart trying to burst out of my chest was the loudest sound in the hallway until Flax, still at my feet, started a low growl.

Helen made a scoffing sound and leaned one shoulder against the wall. 'They haven't gone far, you know, those crows. They're right outside. Wonderful birds, they are. I remember how my mother loved them. So sleek and glossy, such knowing eyes. I bet I could call them in if I tried hard enough.'

'Don't talk to me about your repulsive mother!' snarled Orsa. 'Those stupid birds have been persecuting me for years, even inside! I couldn't cross the courtyard, or sit in the sun, or work in the prison gardens without being pecked half to death. But they won't come inside for anything. Not even your stupid mummy.' She dragged in a noisy breath, her back against the door, glancing at her tame policeman to make sure he still had us covered. 'Now it's time for payback. Where is she?'

Helen and her uncle swapped a look. 'This is all to find my mum?'

'Of course it is! Just tell me where she is and I'll tell you where you can find your snivelling, no-magic, flat little brother!'

The professor snorted. 'You've miscalculated there. None of us knows where Jenny is.'

'Rubbish! I don't believe you! Of course you know where she is.'

'No,' Professor Dartin said. 'Jenny disappeared. We don't have contact with her.'

I could tell from the strained look on Helen's face that this was completely true, but Orsa didn't believe it.

'Don't give me that nonsense! You must know where she is.'

'We don't,' said Helen. 'You threatened her and you threatened all of us, so her only option was leaving to start a new life. She got away from you and all your tame bullies, somewhere you'll never find her.'

As she said this, Helen looked with loathing at the policeman who was supposed to be protecting us.

He flushed red and muttered, 'I can't help it! I have no choice. You don't understand, I owe her.'

Helen put her hands on her hips, frowning awfully. She looked at least ten years older. 'You always have a choice,' she scoffed, 'no matter what anyone threatens. You can choose to honour your family's debt to this murderer, or you can choose to finally put an end to her crimes. Think about it, Constable. Whose side are you on?'

'It's not that easy, missy. You think I want to help her because of the stupid debt my father left me? I have a wife and two little girls. She'd kill them, she would. She's proved it many times. Nobody is safe while she's out!'

'But the police—Oh.' Helen bit her lip. Like me, she was just realising what a long reach the Mussaris must have. If a policeman could be blackmailed into helping her, there was no telling how anyone could be safe.

'Stop right there!' Orsa screeched. 'Stop talking. You, stupid Jenny's girl: just give me a way to find her. What's her new name? Where does she live? Tell me! Tell me, and you can all go back to playing happy families.'

'I don't know,' Helen said. 'I really don't, and I can see now why Mum was so secretive. Nobody can find her, not the authorities, not us, certainly not you. This is over. You're never going to find her.'

Orsa surprised us all then. Instead of ranting or attacking Helen, she pounced on Flax, grabbing him by the scruff as though he was a tiny kitten instead of a ten-kilo Maine Coon. Flax went limp, his mouth open as he struggled to breathe.

Orsa cackled, her face screwed up as tears of hilarity ran down her cheeks. She shook the cat hard, and Flax let out a weak meow.

'Not so smart now, are you, Reynard? And you, Helen-I'm-so-clever-like-my-mum! Who's in charge now?'

I watched in disbelief as Orsa seemed to grow taller and bigger all over, her fingers clenched in the cat's fur becoming all pudgy and swollen. She shook Flax again, and this time he didn't make a sound. I put a hand over my mouth, afraid that she was going to break his neck in front of our eyes.

Just tell me where she is! Orsa screamed, making everyone jump. Helen glared, and I heard her drag in a sobbing breath. Even poor pathetic Constable Maric nearly dropped his gun, but unfortunately he recovered and turned it on us again.

'All of this is your mother's fault, you know, all of it!' Orsa snarled. 'If she'd never stolen Red from me in the first place—'

'Wrong. What nonsense,' the professor interrupted in a dry, strong voice, like he was delivering a lecture. 'Stop this now, before you get yourself into more trouble. Before I call the real police.' He spared a disgusted glance at the constable. 'Orsa, you are completely wrong, and couldn't be more so. Red and

Jenny were together long before you came on the scene. Red was never yours. Never.'

'He was so!' Orsa insisted, still gripping Flax in a chokehold. Her face was as red as a New Year's lantern. 'He should have been! He should have been mine, and they should have been my children, too. What right did Jenny ever have to children, I ask you? All she thought of was her stupid legal aid career. I deserved children much more than she did.'

'You must be completely deranged to think that,' said Professor Dartin, again like he was reading from a list of facts that everyone should know. 'Any person less suited to healthy family relationships than you is impossible to imagine. It's not nice to say it, but you would have made a terrible mother, Orsa.'

While she spluttered and puffed, trying to find a good reply, I saw the professor glance sideways again at the policeman. My heart bounced almost into my throat as I guessed what was coming.

'I would not!' Orsa shouted. 'I would have been marvellous. I would have been the world's best mother ever.'

We all moved within seconds of each other. Professor Dartin threw himself sideways and knocked the pistol out of the policeman's hand. Orsa sprang at the professor, throwing Flax into the air as she did, just where I was able to pull him into my arms. Helen jumped on Orsa's back as she started thumping her opponent, and then the stunned policeman shook himself and looked around for his gun. I saw it at the same instant he did, and we crashed together in a bruising pile of arms and legs as we both went for it. My hand got on it first, and he looked at me like he was going to cry.

That was when I noticed Orsa had pulled out a screwdriver to use as a knife. I yelled a warning, and Helen lifted her foot to stamp down on Orsa's arm.

For the next little space of time, the only noise was all of us gasping for breath, and poor Flax wheezing like my brother Jason in the middle of an asthma attack. He had attached himself firmly to my shoulder, using all his claws. I stepped back from everyone else and concentrated on pointing the gun away from us. One by one, the others stood up, Helen snagging her phone out of her back pocket. While she called triple zero, the rest of us took stock.

'Really? You, a mother?' Professor Dartin asked as if there hadn't just been a violent interruption, but he was puffing a bit, like he'd been running. He got to his feet, standing over Orsa, and shot us a glance. 'Are you all right, Mia? Helen?'

'We're fine,' said Helen, still giving details on her phone. 'Yes please, it's urgent. Thank you.' She cut off the call. All the time Helen was talking, she'd kept her eyes fixed on Constable Maric.

She put her hands on her hips. 'I think you've got a lot of explaining to do, officer, but for now you'd better just keep still and say nothing. You're in such a heap of trouble.'

The policeman looked miserable, but he nodded, not moving from where he huddled on the floor. Orsa growled his way, and he cowered into himself like a beaten puppy. I almost felt sorry for him, but I still kept well away from him. I wasn't going to let him get near his service pistol again.

'Listen to yourself,' the professor said to Orsa. 'Snarling at another person you've bullied and threatened. You, a mother? What about your temper? Your rages? Your utter selfishness? Your inventive ways in cheating, corruption, and bribery? Your violence and your bitterness? Hardly the stuff of solid parenthood, hey?'

Orsa bridled and tried to rise, creeping toward him. 'Rubbish! I would have given those children everything they ever wanted. What sort of mother did she turn out to be, anyway? Your precious Jenny abandoned them.'

Helen had heard enough. She shouted in a fierce voice I had never heard her use. 'Abandoned?' she cried. Flax started in my arms, and I nearly dropped the gun. 'How *dare* you! You drove her off, you evil creature. *You* forced Mum to leave home. *You* persecuted her and threatened everybody she loved. You harassed my dad, and you followed me, and you even tried to run over poor Toby. A six-year-old! You should be ashamed of yourself. Everything my mother did, she did to protect us from *you.*'

'And I guess she succeeded,' Constable Maric said, suddenly sounding more composed. He had one hand on his comms unit. 'Jenny Dartin turned out to be the best guardian of all. We're all safe because Mussari here is going back inside.'

Everyone turned to stare at him. The relief on his face was awesome to see. More static and beeping came from his device, and he murmured back into it.

'What did you just say?' asked Professor Dartin.

'We're safe,' said Constable Maric. He sounded even more relieved than he looked. 'Jenny Dartin wins, and the Mussaris are finished. Your brother's been found, miss; he's safe and well. I'm safe, and my family is safe! Everything's going to be fine.'

We were all stunned, especially poor angry Orsa, who was wailing and crying.

'No, no, no, no!'

The front door was shaken by another loud bang, and it burst open as a squad of armed police rushed through, knocking Orsa aside, filling the space with their large bodies and shouting at us to get down on the ground. I couldn't follow what was happening properly because two of the officers backed me into a corner, yelling at me about the gun, waving their rifles in my face. They wore featureless helmets and body armour and black gloves, and their guns looked huge.

I threw the pistol onto the floor and dropped to my knees,

then put my hands in the air like they told me. Flax was still heavy on my shoulder, his tail high in the air, every strand of his fur fluffed out again, and one of the officers was pointing his gun straight at the big cat.

'No!' I pleaded.

Flax let out a roaring meow, so loud that it obscured all other sounds in the crowded hallway. The officers stepped back, like they were afraid of Toby's cat. We all looked at each other, trying to sort out what was going on.

There was a beat of silence, and I heard the professor politely asking the police to leave me alone.

Then Helen let out a wail. 'She's gone! Where is she?'

Orsa Mussari and her tame policeman were nowhere to be seen.

Outside in the garden, an enormous mob of crows was wheeling and screeching as one of the police vehicles sped off down the driveway.

PART NINE
TOBY

CHAPTER 27

TO FIGHT ANOTHER DAY

I'd never remember everything about that day, but I did recall lying, smothered in blankets and covered with a silver foil wrap, in the back of an ambulance. My whole face started to ache like crazy in the warmth, and I felt like crying with the pain of it, biting my lip instead. My dad was beside me, hovering and blocking the light, holding my hand with tears running down his face. Every now and then, an ambo shepherded him aside and fiddled with something or other—there were any number of tubes in me and patches on me—and the beeping of a monitor steadied at the touch. My dad's hand was very warm. I tried to smile at him, but my face was tight and crusty, feeling kind of swollen but not so painful as the drugs kicked in. My eyelids got very heavy. The up-and-down warble of the siren was somehow comforting, and I discovered that lying on an ambulance trolley was a bit like flying. I felt every jolt when we braked or accelerated or turned, but mostly it was quite soothing, like being rocked to sleep in the white noise of a plane.

Much later, Helen told me that I slept for something like thirty hours, and had two lots of surgery in the middle somewhere. Apparently Orsa had broken my cheekbone as well as my nose. A few little fragments of bone had busted away, so they had to fit some metal wire around my eye socket.

One good result of that was that I'd never be quite so boring-looking as before, with half my face now made of titanium. After a few weeks, I had hardly any scars—a little line near my eyebrow, and a bigger one under my hair at the temple. The surgeons cut through the inside of my mouth too, to get the screws and wires into position. The plastic surgeon was a friend of Dad's who flew down from Sydney especially to do the operation. Not that I knew anything about any of that for quite a while.

When I woke up, Frankie and Helen were sitting beside my hospital bed, mumbling something about coffee and cake. I realised I had a very empty feeling in my stomach, and I wanted to say 'Get some for me too,' except I couldn't talk very well. They heard me trying to speak, and in an instant they were all over me, patting me and telling me so much about what happened that I could hardly follow what they were saying.

'She stole a Jeep to get off the mountain, you see,' Helen said. 'And then she came to threaten us at home. It was terrifying!'

'Not before she'd left your bloody jacket at the police caravan,' Frankie added. 'And I mean bloody! Talk about terrifying. That sure set the cat amongst the pigeons.'

'And Mia grabbed the policeman's gun, and I got the screwdriver off her, just as she was trying to stab Uncle Rain,' said Helen.

'And after that Flax went completely mad, trying to scratch Orsa's eyes out, and screaming like nothing you've ever heard before,' Frankie told me. 'The police had to get Mia to hold him still.'

'And those crows were sent by Mum, do you see?' said

Helen. 'She's had them tracking Orsa for years, ever since she went away. They did a fabulous job. I think I love crows, don't you?'

'I wish they'd kept on tracking her,' Frankie said, at last looking about him and lowering his voice as he realised there were hospital staff within earshot.

I frowned and Helen said quietly, 'She got away, Toby. They're looking for her. Don't worry, she can't hurt you now.'

I had a bit of trouble following what they were talking about, but as they went on, I caught up. After she left me, Orsa went to our house and threatened everyone, and then escaped with a rogue policeman.

I should have been really angry that she got away, but I was just glad she was nowhere near me.

'And she's lost that bracelet,' Frankie said in a kind of stage whisper. 'We've all taken turns looking everywhere we can think of, but there's no sign of it.' He lifted his voice a bit. 'Which reminds me, young Toby, we still don't know where you spent the night. That's another place we can look for the bracelet. Where were you all that time?'

I was still confused and light-headed, so I sort of waved my hand at them, asking them to slow down with the story. There was a bit of shushing and shuffling, then a nurse came and sent them both away for a few minutes while she checked me over. She helped me to sit up a bit and gave me some lemonade, which she made me sip through a straw.

'Not for long,' she told me. 'It's just your cheekbone, not your jaw, so at least your mouth's not wired shut. However, there's a lot of swelling and quite a few stitches inside your mouth. That means you need to be careful for a few days.'

I felt better after she fluffed my pillows and dabbed my face clean with a fresh cloth. She even combed my hair for me before she called my visitors back. I was busy un-sticking my hair from where she'd pasted it flat to my forehead when I noticed something I'd never seen before.

I was wearing a friendship band. Something I'd never worn in my life. Then I remembered the crow cave, all of it: Orsa shrinking down, me putting on the bracelet, the way it fitted itself onto my wrist. I wondered it the medical staff had tried to take it off before surgery, or if maybe they couldn't even see it.

As I frowned at it, holding my hand in front of my face, Helen and Frankie reappeared, behaving a little more respectably, as if finally remembering that they were the adults in the room.

'I asked them to page Dad,' Helen told me. 'And Uncle Rain too.'

'Toby, I know you're tired,' said Frankie, 'but you need to pay attention for a minute. That bracelet is important.' He leaned over me and looked me in the eye, as if making sure I had all my wits about me. 'Listen, Maggie and Barb—you know the vet and her partner—they're going to take their dogs up the mountain to look for that bracelet. Where were you during the night? Where exactly?'

I looked back at him and almost smiled, remembering in time how much it hurt to move my mouth. 'We were at Babylon Rock, you know, on the long track past the waterfall. We were inside the crow cave, at the bottom of the standing stones.'

'Right!' said Frankie, pulling his phone from his back pocket. 'I'll just let Maggie know. The crow cave. On one of the mountain tracks. I've never heard of it, but she might know.'

I made a sound that was a bit odd, because suddenly I felt like laughing aloud and I knew I shouldn't do any such thing with a face wired shut. I reached for Frankie's hand instead.

'But you don't need to bother,' I said, brandishing my wrist. 'It's here! This is it.'

'That's the magic bracelet?' Helen asked doubtfully. 'Are you sure?' Her glance swerved toward the door, as if she wanted to call the nurse back to me. No doubt she thought I'd begun hallucinating.

'Yes. I'm sure,' I answered. 'Just feel it.'

Helen reached forward. The friendship band was an intricate plait of dark grey and silver strands. It looked like cotton, but it felt like metal. As my magical sister touched it, it even gleamed briefly.

'Oho!' Helen said brightly, though there were tears in her eyes. 'I can definitely smell magic. I think my brother's a wizard, after all.'

I opened my mouth to protest. It was the bracelet that was magic, not me. At least I thought so. I didn't dare think otherwise. The bracelet, and Katkin. That was the combination that let me do anything magic.

I didn't want to disappoint my family again by getting their hopes up, so I didn't say anything.

Lucky for me, another visitor arrived just then. Two visitors, the best that could be. I got a whole burst of gladness to see Mia, to see her safe and well. Under cover of coming close to put her hand on mine, she leaned forward, her backpack held awkwardly under one arm. Then the only thing that could make her visit better happened—Katkin squirmed out of the bag and wormed her way under my sheets before any of the staff could spot her.

Tobias Felix! she sang, pressing her cold nose against me. *When will you come home?*

Helen and Frankie saw the sneaky cat, but neither of them could catch what Katkin said.

I thought Mia got the sense of it though, because she smiled and said, 'We're missing you, Toby. When can you come home?'

My face hurt from trying not to smile back at her. I shrugged and took hold of her hand, whispering a soft 'thank you'.

Mia sat beside me until Dad reached my bedside, when she made room for him to come close. He didn't say anything, and neither did I. We just looked at each other, knowing we'd be okay.

Uncle Rain followed a few minutes later, then the nurse came to the doorway and said there were too many visitors and that some of these people had to leave now. Uncle Rain went back down the corridor to work, and Helen and Frankie took Mia and Katkin home. Katkin was not happy about going because she thought she could just stay under the covers, but she cheered up when Frankie said they could go in his little orange car. For some reason, she liked it much better than Dad's big sedan that she came home from the mountain in. Mia promised to come and see me again the next day, and every day until I got home, bringing her secret visitor with her.

They left, and I watched them go out, whispering and giggling about hiding a cat in a backpack in a hospital.

Dad sat down as if he wasn't going anywhere for quite a while, and that was just fine with me. I fell asleep.

When I woke up again, he was still there, and he stayed for a couple more hours. He told me the whole history of him and Mum and Orsa Mussari, and we both got a bit teary when he reached the part about Mum never coming home again, ever. But he kept hold of my hand and I tried to smile at him, despite how tight my face felt. I couldn't say anything, but I thanked him with my look.

It really hurt to smile for the first few days, but everything got better pretty quickly, especially when they discharged me and I got to go home and sleep in my own bed. Hospitals and me were not the best match, I decided.

For another week or so, until my after-surgery checkup, I was pretty much housebound. Most of every day and all of every night, Katkin curled beside me.

I started to rely on having her near me, because I really needed the comfort of her presence and her magic. Every now and then, I shivered in fear when I thought about Orsa Mussari being out there on the run, but we didn't hear anything more from her. Dad and Uncle Rain set up a few magic wards with the help of the crows, and nothing tried to break them.

Weeks went by and the police couldn't track Orsa. The worst news was when they found Constable Maric in Melbourne. Constable Maric was dead. It looked like a suicide, they said officially, but maybe someone pushed him off the platform under the train. We all felt horrible about that. Dad said that at least Orsa had no hold over him now. His family's debt must be paid off in full, but it must have been horrible for his wife and kids.

There was no evidence that Orsa even got as far as Melbourne. I was worried that her ways of hiding were just as good as my mum's, but there was nothing I could do about either of them.

Our rescue cat Tenner and her kittens joined our domestic routine and visited me now and then. They took up with Mia's little brothers while I was away; Jason, August, and Joseph volunteered to help out with the cattery, as we called it, while Dad and Helen and Frankie were doing hospital visits and police statements during that first week. Maggie neutered all the street cats, and now Littlest and Wart spent most of their time in the Lams' house, clambering all over the little boys' bunk beds and generally getting up to mischief.

We never got around to setting up a cat home in the shed. Tenner and her daughters Pink and Footsie usually hung around in our house, and Flax seemed quite happy to surround himself with a clique of female cats. Like me, Flax hadn't quite recovered from his adventure with Orsa. Now he walked like a very old cat, like his joints were aching. He'd dropped quite a bit of weight too, and his beautiful coat was shedding all over the house. Flax was as ancient as Katkin, and Orsa had turned his magic inside out when she tried to use him for power. Katkin said he'd need time to recover, but if he could be quiet and not use his magic for a while, he should be okay.

They'd become very close, those two. All in all, our strange feline set up worked well, and any problems our neighbourhood previously noticed with mice and rats completely disappeared.

By the time summer came around, everything was back to normal—or as normal as it would ever be again. Katkin and I sharpened our magic connection, and I discovered that I actually did have my own magic—not that I made a song and dance about it while I learned to manage it. I just casually mentioned that I'd found out my particular strengths were listening and finding. That was no help with stuff like exams or cooking or parking or most other everyday necessities, but it was actually quite useful to know the whereabouts not only of all the cats who lived with us but of the family members too.

Dad, Helen, and Uncle Rain all nodded when I made this announcement, as if they already knew, but Helen was not the only one with a sparkle in her eye.

Uncle Rain said over and over that he should have guessed I would turn into a listener, given my apparently amazing ability to hear Tenner when even my dad couldn't, and he started advising me to consider different career options—mediator, counsellor, psychologist, and so on. Maybe even teaching, he said. Dad told me I could do whatever I want, the same as he always had. There was a lot to think about, but luckily, there was no need to make any quick decisions. My end-of-year results were good enough for me to aim for any of the courses that Uncle Rain suggested, and I still had a couple of weeks to make my subject choices for the next school year.

For a summer holiday project, Dad and Mia's father helped me remodel my room with a built-in desk, a whole wall of bookshelves, and hooks to hang speakers and screens. That poor deluded policeman had pretty much torn my bedroom apart, looking for some connection to Mum, I guess. When I recovered, I didn't feel right living in a pale blue room with train decals around the walls and a white-painted chest of drawers— the decor my mum chose for my six-year-old self. When my space was finished, the DIY bug had us all looking for something else to tackle, so Dad and I helped Mr Lam enclose their back verandah. That made a bedroom for Mia and Lucky Day to share. Then I helped them put up a new verandah on the back of that.

We were very busy and very happy.

One more odd thing happened at Christmas time. It was after lunch, and we had a gang of people there—Dad, Helen, and me; a Christmas orphan from Helen's office called Timmy; Uncle Rain with his girlfriend Sasha, who was also an emergency specialist; and Maggie and Barb and their elderly and well-behaved springer spaniels, who were smart enough to stay clear of all our cats.

The Lam family came over like they always did on Christmas afternoon, and we were playing a hilarious game of tippety-run cricket when a dark sedan pulled into our driveway.

We were expecting Frankie and his parents in the little orange car, so we were surprised to see Inspector Gray step out and make his way toward us. Then a white ute pulled in behind the sedan, and two blokes in Search and Rescue uniforms emerged. It was Sergeant Miller with his off-sider Adrian Pickles. We hadn't seen any of them since all our depositions at the police station after Orsa got away.

They didn't look worried, so I ordered my racing heart to calm down; it wasn't about Orsa, there was no danger. Katkin seemed on high alert, though, so I wasn't relaxing any time soon.

Anything wrong? I asked her.

She nosed my cheek and kept her eyes fixed on the visitors, like she was waiting to hear what they said. I guessed even an ancient cat stacked full of magic couldn't know everything. Mia sat beside me on the verandah steps and we waited to see what they'd come for.

After all the usual season's greetings and introductions and how-are-yous, Dad started the coffee and cake going, and when we all had what we wanted, Inspector Gray got to the point.

'Sorry to interrupt your Christmas,' he said, 'but I thought you'd like to know there's been a confirmed sighting of Orsa Mussari.'

Luckily, I was already sitting down. Katkin raised a paw and placed it on my hair, like she was telling me to listen calmly, then she jumped off my lap. She joined Flax where he was lying under the outdoor table in the shade. Mia slipped her hand into mine.

Inspector Gray went on. 'She's been hiding out in the east Sydney suburbs, and we got a tip off. Unfortunately, somebody must have told her we were coming because she got away again. I just thought you should know that it's possible she might surface again in the future.'

Of course, none of us could be happy about that, because there was no way we wanted Orsa to come after us or to get away with what she'd done. Sergeant Miller added that he rather thought Orsa wouldn't have much support from her old community. He reckoned she'd chewed through every favour that she might have called in, and now she'd hit rock bottom.

'Unless some idiot in her wider family gets stupid ideas,' he said, 'I think we'll eventually catch up with her.'

We were all really glad to hear this, although it made me suspect that Sergeant Miller must be more connected with the magic world than he let on. Inspector Gray said that as Orsa was facing multiple charges, like theft of a motor vehicle and kidnapping and reckless driving and assault and threatening behaviour and possession of a weapon, and had a history of violent crime on top of her white-collar fraud record, that even with a diagnosis of psychiatric illness she would go away for a very long time when they eventually apprehended her. But for now, he thought Orsa would be too busy hiding to come after any of us.

'I'm only sorry that your mother isn't here, Toby,' Inspector Gray added, looking at our house as if Mum might suddenly appear at one of the windows. 'Jenny Dartin told me ten years ago that she'd make sure you were safe. Looks like she's done it.'

'She has,' said my father. 'I only wish she could be here to know it.'

'I hope she's okay,' Helen added. 'I miss her so much.'

'Me too,' I said. It had been so long that I could only just remember what my mum looked like, even though lately we'd been looking through the old photo albums and putting up pictures of her, some framed snaps that my dad had put away because they used to upset me when I was young. I know that she looked like Helen, and that she used to read me stories every night, but I couldn't quite recall her voice. I hoped she was okay, wherever she was.

Suddenly, Katkin jumped into my arms and pawed my face softly. I rubbed noses with her.

She's well, said Katkin. *Don't you feel it?*

The two of us had been working on our skills, but I'd never thought to look for my mother, either with my listening or my finding. Despite the December heat, I felt a shiver go down my spine. Could it be that easy? I turned away from the conversation and thought about it. In a few moments, I could *find* everyone in our family, like Mia beside me and even Frankie as he backed his car out of his parents' driveway.

So I looked a bit harder, thinking about my mum.

I couldn't find her.

I couldn't find her; she was behind a wall of shimmer. Whatever hiding place she found, she'd reinforced it with magic wards.

Then suddenly I could hear her. It was her! I locked onto her voice and it was perfect; it was exactly as it should be. In my head, I could hear her speaking aloud and she sent an overwhelming sense of her love for us and her thoughts about us, and though I couldn't say exactly what words she used, they struck me deeply and I knew that everything I was feeling was true and real and happening now, a precious piece of everyday magic. I could tell that Mum was healthy and content, somewhere, working for other people like she always did, and thinking of us.

That's it, said Katkin. *She'll never be far away.*

I sent my love and thanks, and I hope she heard me.

Acknowledgments

No book springs to life fully formed. *How to Survive Your Magical Family* is no exception, although Toby's story downloaded its first event in a particularly vivid dream: the street cat accident!

From that day to this has been quite the journey, with many helping hands (and paws) along the way.

Thanks again to my early readers Kate Maher and Aveline Pérez de Vera, and to Damian Sweeney and family for their support and suggestions. I'm grateful to Robyn Starkey for her advice on feline matters ... I suspect she has cat magic herself.

Like Toby, I love cats but I'd describe myself as more of a dog person. My writing companion is decidedly canine, and she regularly demands attention with a paw swipe. This book is inspired by the cats in my life, including Rocky, Daisy, and more recently Nico.

Last, thanks to my husband, family, and friends for their love and support, and to Michelle Lovi at Odyssey Books for taking on another novel of mine in yet another genre. I'm very proud of our partnership.

Long may we create adventures together.

ABOUT THE AUTHOR

Clare Rhoden writes thoughtful adventures with heart and soul. Known for her immersive world-building and relatable characters, Clare's books tell of hope and love in the darkest times.

Clare lives in Melbourne Australia with her husband and her very clever spoodle.

Clare's novels are published by Odyssey Books.

You can find out more at www.clarerhoden.com

facebook.com/clarerhoden

instagram.com/clarerhodenauthor

bookbub.com/authors/clare-rhoden

goodreads.com/clarerhoden